ELIZABETH

A Holy Land Pilgrimage

Cheryl Dickow

Bezalel Books
Waterford, MI

Published by
Bezalel Books
Waterford, MI

Printed in the United States of America

For information on Bezalel Books, to purchase other books by Cheryl Dickow, or to ask Cheryl to speak at your event, please visit www.BezalelBooks.com

Library of Congress Control Number: 2006911237

ISBN 978-0-9792258-0-2

FIRST FRUITS

The choicest first fruits of your soil you shall bring to the house of the Lord, your God.

Exodus 23:19

But now Christ has been raised from the dead, the first fruits of those who have fallen asleep.

1 Corinthians 15:20

 As the first fruits of Bezalel Books, this book, "Elizabeth: A Holy Land Pilgrimage," is offered to the Lord, my God.

Cheryl Dickow

Chapter One

*Keep me safe, O God; in you I take
refuge. Psalm 16:1*

The easiest decision Beth ever made was to
take this vacation. Having just turned forty-eight
and smack dab in the middle of her very own mid-life
crisis, she knew she needed to get away. Her children
were now teenagers and could, essentially, fend for
themselves. In truth, given her disposition of late,
they had long been fending for themselves. Her
husband, both loving and frustrating at the same
time, had given his blessings for this trip. He didn't
even flinch when she shared with him her interest in
spending time in Israel.

Luke had long ago understood that Beth's
fascination with the Jewish roots of their faith was
unquenchable. Their home library was filled with
books from the Talmud to the Torah. Books written
in Hebrew cast a spell over Beth and she sought
them in every bookstore she entered, in every yard
sale she perused. The two small, quaint bookstores
within a three mile radius of their home had become
Beth's favorite haunts on the first Saturday of every
month with shelves stocked in new arrivals.

As she drove the twenty miles from her home
to the airport she thought of her husband's easy
acceptance of her grand plans. She had to wonder if
he wanted her out of the house as much as she
wanted to get out. Wouldn't that be something? But
she was too determined to escape to even take issue
with that interesting prospect. But now, as she
approached her gate, she realized how unfettered this
whole undertaking had been. When she first

introduced the idea to Luke, she was only mid-way through her rehearsed discourse on why this was the ideal plan when she was struck by the absurdity of her own words. Here she was, in all seriousness, explaining to Luke why Israel was the perfect choice for time to herself, when she realized she didn't even have a passport. Never had. And now she wanted to go to Israel! She really got a kick out of herself sometimes and could see her kids shaking their heads in mock support of their dad, who most certainly seemed to have his hands full with Beth.

Parking in the long term parking lot, she waved down the shuttle and adroitly joined the other passengers, all silently contemplating their day's events. Before she knew it, she was at the airport and following the signs that gently guided her towards the correct line. As she took her place behind an older couple arguing about where they should keep their long term parking lot ticket, she imagined herself ensconced in the apartment she had rented in the heart of Jerusalem. She could envision the peace and tranquility that would be hers. All hers. No kids demanding to be fed and no laundry piles snickering at her inability to claim victory. She was sure that Luke, her equally beleaguered husband, knew better than to let the laundry pile up while she was gone.

He wouldn't dare let her come home from a peaceful, relaxing vacation to walk into all that she had said she was running from: unending demands. She didn't allow herself to feel guilty because, with their oldest son off to college, the only laundry that Luke would have to contend with was his own and that of the other three children. And cooking was something that Luke enjoyed. Sophia, their daughter, was a junior in high school and the apple of her father's eye. They both enjoyed each other's company and she seemed to be following in his footsteps in the culinary department. They often cooked together, sometimes in complete silence. Sophia created meat rubs while Luke whipped up barbeque sauces that would rival anything on the supermarket shelves.

Yes, Luke probably wanted Beth out of the house as much as she wanted to get out of the house. Nonetheless, Beth smiled as she secretly hoped that Luke would both enjoy his time with Sophia, Joseph, now a high school freshman, and Sammy, a sweet natured seventh grader, but also struggle with her absence. Beth prayed that Luke would realize that she was the best thing that had ever happened to him. She hadn't felt valued in quite a while and she could no longer distinguish if it was coming from her marriage or from life in general.

Undoubtedly, she needed some time to herself, she thought, as she waited in line, ticket in hand, and her tote filled with the three books she had planned on reading. She had two beautiful weeks stretching ahead of her and eagerly anticipated reading from the moment she boarded her first flight to New York all the way to catching her second plane to Israel. Although at that very moment in time she was sorely regretting the particularly heavy novels as they weighed her down and caused her neck muscles to strain. She couldn't get on board fast enough.

Check-in went a whole lot smoother than she had expected. Luke convinced her to arrive two and a half hours before her flight's scheduled departure. With age, his conservatism had reached new heights. Where once she found him a "rock" and a "safe harbor," she now found him aggravating. Or, as their counselor had corrected, it wasn't Luke that Beth found aggravating, it was his "ways." Beth shook her head at the time and money they had chosen to pay in fees to a marriage counselor. She wasn't sure that either had been well spent, but there it was, done. She wasn't going to mope over it.

Initially, Beth was convinced that new window coverings and a couple of wing back chairs would have suited her better than counseling. But that seemed selfish in the face of the ice age that had settled in her house. So she and Luke made a few phone calls and decided to begin therapy. Maybe it had accomplished something. Who knows? When Luke and Beth had originally agreed that they needed a mediator in their relationship, Beth had felt they were very much on the verge of a divorce. She was tired and more than ready to throw in the towel. Divorce ran in Beth's family like red hair and freckles ran in other families.

She had to admit that they learned to talk nicer to each other, and that was certainly beneficial. They learned rules about not attacking one another but keeping their focus on the issues at hand. Beth was notorious for remembering the pains that Luke had inflicted upon her in their early years of marriage while Luke was good at the kind of general insults that had a way of festering in Beth's heart and mind. Beth walked sideways down the aisle of the plane, searching for her seat, as she remembered their first session.

"So, I believe the best place to begin is to hear what each of you feels is the reason for being here and what you would like to get out of this time together."

Sitting on a beautiful tapestry couch, Beth did everything in her power not to roll her eyes at the therapist sitting across from her. How ironic that the therapist was sitting in a wing back chair, now only a distant hope for Beth as her extra money went to these sessions. All Beth could think of was, *Look at her in that gorgeous wing back chair! That's what I really wanted,* but instead she said, "Luke and I have been struggling with being kind to each other. We are here because we have a twenty year marriage we would like to salvage and four children to whom we want to provide a warm and loving home." Beth sat and waited for either Luke or the therapist to speak. She didn't really care which one took a turn, she felt she had risen to the occasion and was quite pleased with herself.

Shifting in her chair so that she could more squarely face Luke, the therapist asked, "Luke, what do you see as the reason you are here and your goals?"

Never a man of many words, Beth was as curious as Ms. Claireborne, their counselor, about Luke's response, maybe even more so. Beth, then, turned to face Luke and was reminded how very much she was still attracted to her own husband. He was just under six feet tall and fairly thin, at least compared to most fifty-something men she met. He had magnificent arms that always made her tingle when she looked at them. She loved to watch him work in the summer, mowing the lawn or washing the cars. His muscles were well defined and he had great strength in his arms. She remembered when she was pregnant with their first son and had sprained her ankle. Luke had carried her around their little apartment for two days because she could not put any weight on her foot without a tremendous amount of pain. And, being pregnant, she was unable to take any pain medicine. Luke picked her up as if she had been as light as a feather.

When Luke spoke, Elizabeth caught a breath in her throat as she heard him use her name. Lately, there had been very little in the way of closeness between the two of them and hearing Luke's familiarity with her name made her heart skip a beat. He was the only person alive who called her "Liz." The most common derivative of Elizabeth was Beth, and that was how everyone addressed her except, of course, her mother, who only used her formal, given name. Beth always got a kick out of her mother's pronunciation: Eee-liz-a-beth. It was as if it was the single, most beautiful name on the planet and it would be a sin to slur any of the syllables together. But there Luke was, using his special name for his wife. "Like Liz said, we've both been having a difficult time speaking kindly to one another and neither of us feels this is the kind of home we want our children to be raised in."

Well, we finally agree on something! Beth thought as Luke concluded his response. How absurd that their first agreement in ages should be at a marriage counselor's office.

Beth was jarred back to reality when she realized she had walked down the entire length of the plane without locating her seat. Daydreaming had become a real problem of late. Pretending she was interested in a magazine, she rifled through the magazine rack against the back wall of the plane and, feigning disinterest in all that it held, walked back up the aisle to find her seat: J2.

Pitiful behavior for a forty-eight year old woman was all Beth could think as she buckled herself into her seat and opened her tote bag. She purchased it after the completion of their marriage counseling. It was a deep red and green floral pattern with forest green leather straps. If she didn't get anything else out of the sessions she did learn that she loved tapestry, having spent more than a dozen hours on the finely woven embroidered couch at the therapist's office.

She admired the bag and then began wondering how she could have walked right past her seat, lost in her own thoughts. What was she going to be like when she was seventy? Would her children have to be called because she was lost or confused? Sophia's frustration with Beth was becoming ever more apparent as she was growing into a beautiful young woman with ideas of her own. Sometimes Beth felt as if Sophia would have been fine without her and at other times Beth felt that Sophia's confidence came from the knowledge that her mother was her stalwart companion, ever available should Sophia need or want her. And, of course, Sophia neither seemed to need nor want her mother much anymore. She was her own young woman and Beth was tremendously proud of her but often ached at the knowledge that Sophia already had one foot out the door.

Beth shook her head at herself and rummaged through her tote looking for her novel. These were all thoughts she wanted to leave behind right now. Viewing the contents of her bag, she saw three small plastic dispensers of tissue, a couple packs of cinnamon gum, her reading glasses, her sunglasses, and a few protein bars. She could see that Luke had thrown in a plastic bag filled with nuts and raisins. That was Luke, always taking care of everyone. Her friends never understood her frustration at such a man. She tried to explain that, at times, she almost felt like she had no role in the house. Luke could cover everything, and often did.

There, towards the bottom of the tote, she spotted her book. She had purposely selected a longer novel for the first read of her vacation, knowing full well that she would easily be able to immerse herself in such a story. It was about a mountain expedition that was supposed to be filled with mystery, intrigue, and relationships. Rumor had it that it was being made into a movie with two of today's hottest stars. Beth had no interest. She preferred reading a novel and letting her imagination soar. There was very few times where a movie failed to disappoint her when compared to a book.

Her second book was a lighter read, last year's bestseller that she never got around to reading. From what her friends said, more fluff than bulk, but sometimes a girl just needed fluff. The trend was for well known authors to write everything, whether or not it was in their genre. The whole world was about money, both the making and the spending of it. It made her feel old as she often wondered where everyone's values had gone. She lamented the world that her children were inheriting and was glad they had the energy to put up a good fight.

Her last book was really more of a "filler" book in that it could be picked up at any time and simply opened and read. It was a book of Psalms. Beth loved the words as they reflected her own conversations with God.

With her first book in hand, she zipped up her tote and pushed it under the seat in front of her. She couldn't see the occupant but knew that by the time she had worked her way back up the aisle, all the seats and every overhead bin had been filled. It was a good thing she hadn't needed any of that space because it was long gone by the time she claimed her seat.

Putting her head back and closing her eyes, Beth listened to the engines and felt the slight sway of the plane that always made her feel like she were on a ferris wheel ride that was coming to an end. Since menopause she had become extremely sensitive to many sounds and slight movements. She didn't like it when her children plopped themselves on the couch next to her or when they dropped the silverware in the drawer as they emptied the dishwasher. Beth felt as if her nerves were like downed electrical wires, jumping all over the street.

Sophia's room had also become a real issue in the past year. Beth was tired of the piles of clothes on the floor and the complete disregard for Beth's desires to have quiet in the evening hours. There seemed to be a stream of kids coming and going and Beth wanted to scream, *I want quiet!*

Menopause had also added ten pounds to her waist that, try as she might, refused to vanish. She understood what women meant when they moaned; *I gave him the best years of my life.* She couldn't imagine who would be interested in dating her, should she and Luke truly split up. She had literally given him the best years of her life.

Life, that fleeting existence, sure had a way of getting to her lately. She kept her eyes closed and brought to mind the beautiful apartment that she had rented for these next two weeks. She had worked for a travel agency during her last year of college, many moons ago, and she had used them to plan and book this trip. She didn't want to take any chances on using the Internet and end up in some terrible situation, halfway across the globe, alone. She didn't mind paying for the luxury of the peace of mind she had in knowing that her vacation had been in the hands of professionals.

Too many people, she thought, considered themselves experts in all fields but yet didn't think anyone else could do their particular job! Beth was not a travel agent; she was a middle school teacher in a small private school in the suburbs of Detroit. She would leave the travel planning in the hands of professionals and wished that everyone else would do the same for her. She was always amazed at how many parents thought they could do her job, and felt free to tell her just that. Yes, she definitely needed this vacation.

"Ladies and Gentlemen, we have been given the "go-ahead" to depart. Please turn off all cell phones, laptops, and any other electrical devices until we are in the air and you have been given instructions that you may turn them on. We ask that you remain seated during our flight and that, while you are in your seats, you keep your seatbelts on. We expect to arrive in New York as scheduled."

Perfect, thought Beth, as she smiled and drifted off to sleep.

Chapter Two

Listen to my prayer, spoken without guile. Psalm 17:1

Beth awoke, startled, as her book slipped from her lap and landed on her feet. She was sure she had been snoring, another symptom of menopause, and embarrassedly looked at her seat companions. Fortunately, they, too, were older and probably couldn't even hear Beth's snores above the roar of the engines. Beth saw that she missed her chance at a drink and pressed the "call" button for a flight attendant. Normally she would have just dealt with her dry mouth but today felt it necessary to make a statement that the next two weeks were all about her. Not in a rude or offensive way, just her own simple acknowledgement that she, too, was worth the effort.

"Can I help you?" asked the flight attendant as he reached across her seat to turn off the call button.

"Yes, please, I'm sorry that I missed the drink cart. Could I please get a glass of ice water?"

"Sure, just give me a moment," was his reply. Beth refused to feel guilty as he looked up and down the aisle, apparently preparing a strategy to obtain this errant drink requested by a demanding passenger. Of course Beth knew that receiving the drink was only the first leg of the imposition. When she had finished her drink, she knew she would have to press the call button again to dispose of the plastic cup and shards of ice that remained. She opened her book and began reading to indicate that this wasn't something she was going to back down from, regardless of the flight attendant's dramatic flair.

When the plane touched down in New York, Beth had just finished the third chapter of the book. So far, so good. It was just what she had hoped and knew she had made a good decision. The christening flight of her trip was a success. She listened as the pilot instructed everyone to remain seated during the approach to the terminal and filled them in on the weather conditions and time in New York.

Beth had a few hours before her second flight and decided to be one of those people who simply sat in their seats while the other passengers jostled for a place in the aisle, just to stand, like sardines, until the door was opened. This made two very unlike-Beth acts within the space of a few short hours. First, she did not beg off with her interest in a glass of water the moment she saw it would take a bit of maneuvering and now, staying seated during the plane disembarkment, as if she were a lady of leisure. She was practically a new woman already! This was going to be an awesome two weeks.

With the entire airline industry on its head since the fateful September day in 2001, Beth found that safety measures seemed no different entering the El Al terminal than for her flight to New York. Precautions were in place everywhere and everyone was prepared for the eventual questioning by security personnel or the inevitable ransacking of bags and carry-on luggage. Rules, procedures, and limitations were constantly being updated. Currently, you were not allowed to have any beverages, shampoo, creams, or lotions in your carry-on bags. Beth wasn't deterred by any of the edicts. She was too caught up in realizing her longtime dream of visiting Israel for her spirits to be hampered.

As she walked the terminals in New York she felt they, too, were no different than the terminals in Detroit. There were shops touting souvenirs of "The Big Apple" just as Detroit had souvenirs of "The Motor City" or of "Motown," although these were both monikers that Detroit had long ago outgrown. New York also had the same small eateries as in Michigan. There was a restaurant selling hamburgers with its lines spilling out into the halls while the establishments promoting more exotic cuisine seemed quite a bit emptier.

If everyone was like Beth, which she came to realize was more than likely, a tourist was bound to avoid foods with potentially negative long-term effects. "Passing-through" would have been applicable to the person as well as the meal. With an aging population, Beth knew this must be the case for many people and felt a twinge of sadness that she couldn't partake in any of their interesting edibles. Those days were a thing of the past.

By far, Beth's favorite thing to do was people watch. With some time stretching before her, she took a seat and scanned the terminal. She was fascinated by the sheer number of people who inhabited the earth. She often wondered, as she watched people go by, why this one or that one wasn't in her realm of acquaintances. Did God have a master plan and people only met when He deemed it necessary and providential? It was at times like this that Beth drove herself crazy.

Beth opened her bag and took out her book of Psalms. She also removed the bag of nuts and dried fruit that Luke had so thoughtfully packed. She decided to spend some time reading through the calming words and enjoying a light snack. After departing the plane she had stopped and purchased a bottle of cranberry juice. She now opened it and placed it on the seat by her snack. Opening her book, Beth was soon lost in the beauty of King David's words. After some time, Beth's attention was diverted by a commotion she caught in the corner of her eye.

She watched a young mother struggle with a two year old who clearly wanted the cartoon doll in a gift shop. The mother had made the grave mistake of running into the gift shop probably hoping to buy a pack of gum and a magazine and walked out with nothing more than a screaming toddler, arms outstretched, as if the doll could save him from some terrible fate that waited. Beth thought of the countless times she had attempted some excursion with her own children, each endeavor meeting with defeat.

As Beth watched the mother's control slowly slip away, she wondered if she was supposed to go help. Was this woman, at the edge of her patience, meant to be someone whom Beth should know? These were the things Beth grappled with now. Almost too anxious to hear God's call, she often wondered if she had become deaf to it. Sitting in her seat, waiting to be called for boarding, Beth decided this woman wasn't supposed to be in Beth's world. At least not in the physical sense. She decided to quietly say a prayer for the return of the young mother's patience.

As soon as Beth finished her short but heartfelt prayer, her row was called. Securing her tote bag under her left arm, and holding her boarding pass in her right hand, she took her place in line. She smiled at everyone who looked her way, wanting to strike up a conversation with them all. Were they as excited as she was to be traveling to the Holy

Land? She could feel her stomach doing flip-flops at the prospect of standing on the ground that her Lord and Savior stood upon. Were His words still echoing in the foothills of Mount Sinai? Would she feel Judge Deborah's presence at Mount Tabor? Would she break down during her own walk on the Via Dolorosa?

Her questions filled her mind as she inched her way closer to the airplane that would be arriving at Ben Gurion Airport in Tel Aviv in ten hours. For one fleeting moment she wished that Luke were with her. Would he add to her excitement and anticipation or would he detract from it? It was something she hadn't been willing to risk as she weighed the pros and cons of what she felt she needed during the planning portion of this trip.

Part of her thought they needed time together. They could have made arrangements for the two youngest boys to stay with friends and family. Making arrangements for Sophia would have been even easier. But the other part of her, and as it turned out, the larger portion, knew she simply needed time to herself. And it needed to be time that had great meaning for her. Her ache for what life hadn't yet held was becoming almost unbearable at times. Her need to grasp at the tailwinds of time began in earnest the day her son was accepted to college. She watched him read his congratulatory letter and simultaneously saw him as a toddler putting his first puzzle together. Where had the time gone? A searing pain ran through her like a hot knife through butter, melting everything it touched. She couldn't bear to think of Sophia leaving in another year. Two of her children on their own!

Where had *her* life gone became the bigger question. What happened to her dreams of teaching at a local college or of having taken one or two significant family vacations? Time was running through her fingers like sand in an hour glass and each grain became a tear of remorse or regret or fear. She could no longer tell. And so her plan began hatching.

She became fixated on reports that said that a person's forties were the new thirties. By those calculations she was only thirty-eight! This was math that she liked. She found great comfort in that. Thirty-eight was quite young and a great age to take a trip. Once she had recaptured the past ten years, she had to decide on what kind of trip she would take. Her cousin had just returned from France and England. Beth listened intently to stories and enjoyed all the pictures and yet none of it stirred a desire in Beth's heart. The pictures of the Eiffel Tower at night were truly magnificent as were the expensive, melt-in-your-mouth chocolates that Anthony had purchased for everyone. But still, Beth had no inclination to visit those parts of Europe.

Later that week, Beth was writing down everyone's dental appointments on her calendar when her eye caught the calendar's notes for Yom Kippur and Sukkot. In that instant she knew where she was going: Israel. Her childhood memories of growing up in a predominately Jewish neighborhood and having attended more than a few Hanukah parties and synagogue services came flooding back. She wanted to be in Israel. Actually, more accurately, she felt as if she *needed* to be in Israel. And her planning began.

Beth was next in line. She took a step forward and felt as if she were walking with God for the first time in a long time. She was overcome with peace as she moved through the vacuous tunnel to the plane.

This time she was focused on finding her seat and refused to get caught up in any of her day dreams. *S3, S3, S3, S3,* Beth repeated, until she was buckled in. She found that there were great benefits to paying attention.

She selected a nice, clean, freshly folded blanket and a crisply covered pillow from the empty, overhead bin. She easily moved into her seat and got herself situated. Although she wasn't quite ready to make use of her pillow or blanket she was relying on her cousin's advice: *Sleep during your flight, even if you don't want to! You must do everything you can to make it through the first day of your trip without succumbing to sleep. Get yourself on schedule right away.* Her cousin had explained that staying up during this flight, and then sleeping when you arrived at your destination, really threw a wrench in your whole trip. So Beth planned on following her cousin's sage advice and doing her best to get to sleep as soon as they were in the air.

The woman for whom Beth had offered a prayer now stood in the aisle eyeing her ticket and the numbers posted on the small plastic signs above each row. She looked at Beth, her toddler asleep in her arms. Beth smiled knowingly as the woman moved in such a way as to not wake up her child. Beth helped by removing the diaper bag from the woman's shoulder and placing it on the floor, just tucked under the seat enough so that the woman could maneuver her way into the narrow space. Beth watched as the woman bent forward, ever-so-slightly, and then put the palm of her hand against her child's beautiful head so that it wouldn't lunge backward causing him to wake up.

The woman thoughtfully eyed the armrest between her seat and the seat of her toddler. Beth instinctively knew it would be best to raise the armrest to create one large single space for both mother and child versus two small spaces. Beth reached over and in one movement pushed in the release button of the armrest while pulling it up to be tucked between the seatbacks. The mother smiled her appreciation, both women understanding the need for silence. Beth's heart filled with gratitude to the Lord for having allowed her to pray for this mother and her child and for also giving her seat companions that would help her follow her cousin's advice: to sleep.

The plane was in the air, the young mother and her child were serenely tucked into their roomy seat. They were all on their way to Israel. Beth's last cognizant thoughts, as she drifted off to sleep, were from the book of Jeremiah. *For thus says the Lord: Shout with joy for Jacob, exult at the head of the nations; proclaim your praise and say; The Lord has delivered his people, the remnant of Israel. Behold, I will bring them back from the land of the north; I will gather them from the ends of the world, with the blind and the lame in their midst, The mothers and those with child; they shall return as an immense throng.*

Chapter Three

*If I forget you, Jerusalem, may my right
hand wither. Psalm 137:5*

Beth slept fitfully, but that wasn't anything
new. Another bi-product of menopause. Beth sneered
at articles touting the joys of post-menopausal life.
So far, she wasn't a believer. And she was sure that
the onset of this time in her life coinciding with her
son's departure to college didn't do much to add to
her ability to cope. She had to admit that the Lord
must have a tremendous amount of confidence in her
to spring this all on at once. Either that or He had a
great sense of humor!

At one point during her restlessness, Beth
opened her eyes to see the woman in the next seat
feeding the little guy some dry cereal. Both seemed
quite content and Beth started wondering if they
were Americans on their way to Israel for a visit with
friends or family, or if they were Israelis having just
spent time in America. Or, were they Palestinians or
Lebanese or Muslim? Actually, the realm of
possibilities made Beth want to giggle, something
that would have mortified Sophia. Beth was
somewhat dismayed at how easily her daughter
seemed to be embarrassed by Beth's words and
actions. Right now, though, it didn't matter. Beth
felt as if she was on an adventure of a lifetime. It
was better than anything she had ever read, with
limitless possibilities. And she wasn't going to let
anything get in her way.

Beth watched as the mother fed her youngster
and smoothed his hair, while he turned his face

upwards and looked at his mother with deep brown eyes. Whoever they were, their loving actions and gestures towards one another revealed to Beth that family commitment was universal. Just as quickly as Beth's curiosity about their nationality invaded her thoughts, it left. And in its wake was the understanding that love transcended all labels that the world might wish to impose on one another. And then Elizabeth was fast asleep.

The pilot's voice called out to Beth in her dreams but she couldn't rouse herself enough to pay attention. She didn't have any sense of landing gear coming down and refused to be awakened by the general comments regarding time and weather conditions. She moved her pillow from the left side of her head to her right, rolled her head on top of it, and went back to her dreams.

It was a beautiful spring day. The weather was warm, the wind blowing gently through the newly sprouted leaves. The sun warmed her skin and she took off her lightweight jacket. She didn't need it as she bent down to begin work on her garden. She was inspecting last year's growth on a few bushes while deciding where to plant the early blooming larkspur plants. She loved their tall spikes and the gorgeous rose, pink, and lavender colors that she had selected. She knew what magnificent arrangements these made when cut and brought indoors and was already anticipating the centerpieces she would be able to construct. She finally decided to place the larkspur behind her dwarf morning glories. She thought the contrast of heights and colors would be perfect.

As she began digging, her spade hit something hard. She bent forward to get a closer look as she used her fingers to gently pull the dirt away from the hard substance. She seemed to know that the spade would scratch or ruin whatever it was that she had discovered. Like an expert archeologist uncovering the find of the century, she brushed back the dirt to find an oval shaped rock. She picked it up and was stunned to catch a glimpse of the sun's rays reflecting off the tiniest of spots that was free from dirt. She brushed at that small spot and almost dropped the treasure when she realized that it might be a diamond. She looked around to see if anyone was watching and then ran to her home.

She rushed into the small mudroom adjacent to the garage where there was a sink and ran the water over the rock. It *was* a diamond! As it caught the light from the ceiling, it sparkled unlike anything she had ever seen. She stood holding the diamond and, as always, woke up.

Beth had been having this dream for well over a year now. Every few months it became more vivid, more detailed. Each time it progressed a bit more as if it were a story slowly, almost painfully, revealing itself, much to the frustration of Elizabeth. *What are you saying to me?* She would moan upon waking. The first time she had the dream she had just been standing in the garden and could literally feel the sun's warmth on her face. The next time she had the dream she was gathering gardening tools. After that one, was the one where she was contemplating the arrangement of the plants. There had been a few more since then, but now this one was incredible! It now felt complete except for the fact that she was still clueless as to its meaning. And here she was, on her way to Israel. What did it all mean?

"Ladies and gentlemen, we are approaching Ben Gurion Airport in Tel Aviv." He continued on but Elizabeth's thoughts were more pressing than his announcements. Why, in heaven's name, would the dream finally come to completion on her trip to Israel? She was both frustrated and intrigued when she looked out the window and was overcome with emotion. Tears welled up in her eyes and would not stop their journey until they were falling, quite consistently, down her cheeks and onto her lap. Although their origin was a mystery to her, Elizabeth welcomed their release. She knew they had been a long timing coming. She felt a small pressure on her arm and looked down. The little boy next to her had placed his small hand on her sleeve. When she looked at him, he said, "It will be okay." And she knew it would.

Chapter Four

Peace upon Israel!
Psalm 129:6

The rush of emotions that engulfed Elizabeth as she stepped off the plane was overwhelming. She was glad she had spent time visiting miscellaneous friends of friends and various sundry relations who had previously made a trip to Israel. Wanting her experience to be less "touristy" and more "native" had really driven Beth to acquire information in the months leading up to her excursion to the Holy Land. She was thankful for the time that these many strangers had afforded her as she questioned and cajoled information out of each and every person. It was how she had made the decision to rent an apartment instead of staying at a hotel. She liked the idea of living in a neighborhood for the duration of her stay and decided to sacrifice some amenities to do just that.

When she thought of her trip she always envisioned spending time with the people who lived in Israel versus lying at the pool of a hotel with more people like herself. Her sister thought she was crazy to give up the luxuries that would be hers at a hotel while her husband shared his concerns regarding her safety in a neighborhood instead of a hotel. But she was not deterred. And now she was stepping right into her carefully laid plan of living in an apartment on Azza Street in Jerusalem.

With her claimed luggage quietly rolling behind her, she stood ready to exit the Ben Gurion Airport and hail a cab. She wanted to reach her apartment and drop her things off. The young couple from whom she was renting the flat had assured her that a key would be left with their neighbors, the Goldfarbs. Beth was also told that Mr. and Mrs. Goldfarb, while somewhat nosey and more than a bit geriatric, would be a great resource for anything Elizabeth might need, including a warm smile and a hot cup of chicken soup.

Beth tingled with anticipation as she walked out into the warm October air. It was about sixty-five degrees with mostly sunny skies. The Lord could not have given her a more perfect first day in Israel. She knew the Mediterranean was about a half hour away from the airport but was convinced she could smell the sea air. She untied her sweater from around her waist and pushed her arms through. She buttoned the three bottom buttons, as was her habit, and was on her way.

Having read up on all the modes of transportation available; bus, train, cab, and car, she opted for a cab from the airport and then considered using a bus or train for most of her other transportation needs. There were bus stops everywhere, with one even located right in front of her building. While she had been quizzing all of the friends of her friends and even their relatives about trips to Israel she had come across quite a few differing opinions on things. One insisted she eat at this particular outdoor café while another shuddered at such a suggestion. Someone else directed her to shop at this specific shuk, which was an outdoor market, just as another person weighed in with their thoughts about the freshness, or lack thereof, of the cheese found there.

Elizabeth found that her planning was as exhilarating as her proposed trip and immensely enjoyed these information gathering sessions. But regardless of the differing opinions about restaurants, theatres, attractions, and shopping, every single person agreed that she should avoid renting a car. Apparently even the most adept native drivers became lost in the maze of streets and often found themselves facing a dead end because of one misread sign or miscalculation. Based on some of Elizabeth's experiences during these conversations, she secretly figured that the drivers probably got so caught up in trying to make some point or another to their passenger, that they simply missed exits and turns. For Beth, it was one of the quaintest things she could imagine.

During this entire fact finding mission, Beth knew that Luke was keeping his concerns about her safety to an occasional comment or raised eyebrow. She made a point to allay his fears by sharing her newly acquired knowledge and her thought process for most decisions. He seemed to appreciate her thoughtful handling of these important aspects of her trip and she found a sense of pleasure in respecting his concern. She stood under the beautiful skies of Israel, inhaled the aroma of the Mediterranean Sea and listened to the honking and yelling of drivers whizzing by her, barely keeping a respectable distance from the curb.

She smiled and gave thanks to the Lord for His hand in her decision about a cab. She waited until there was a big enough break in traffic before approaching a cab. She picked the driver who looked like he had the most compassionate eyes and left the rest up to God.

Lamely, Elizabeth produced the sounds that she hoped resembled her desire to get to the King David apartments. The driver's eyes twinkled as the corners of his mouth turned upwards in a smile. She then said, "He'dlaktah?" upon situating herself in the cab. She was given this sage advice from all who had recommended cabs. Apparently the drivers were required, by law, to begin their meters as soon as they began the trip. 'He'dlaktah' meant, *Did you start the meter?*

However, most disregarded this law and did their earnest best to simply collect a five dollar fare. Although this seemed more than reasonable to Beth, she understood that she couldn't start doling out five dollars three and four times a day when the actual fare, should the meter be running, would be more like two or three dollars. Plus, in keeping with the new and improved Elizabeth, she was making a statement with that simple question, *He'dlaktah?* While the literal question was an inquiry to the running of the meter, the subliminal question was *Who do you think is in charge?* And the answer she was looking for was, *Elizabeth.*

Beth arrived to her apartment none the worse for wear but had to admit that the streets and traffic were a bit more treacherous than she had anticipated. She knew that maneuvering a car through the congestion and craziness of the streets would have been impossible and was doubly thankful that she didn't talk herself into trying. She paid the cab fare and walked into the apartment building. The apartment she would be staying in was on the third floor and Beth gratefully caught sight of an elevator.

Wheeling her luggage across the warm, tiled floor created clacking sounds that drew the attention of a couple leaving the building. They looked across the mezzanine at Beth and nodded while they said, in unison, "Shalom."

For the first time in her life Beth was tongue-tied as her enthusiasm garbled her response, "Oh-my-gosh-slahom!" This was not at all what Beth had expected from herself and rolled her eyes as the elevator doors closed, but not fast enough for the thoroughly embarrassed Elizabeth. *Slahom! Great job, Beth,* she said to herself during the quick ride to the third floor. *Great job! You should go into politics with your charming social graces.*

Shaking off her humiliation, Beth walked down the narrow hallway towards her apartment, shalosh, apartment three. She was told that across the hall from her apartment would be apartment four, arba, where she would find the Goldfarbs. *Shalosh, arba, shalosh, arba, shalosh, arba.* Elizabeth kept counting as if these two numbers, three and four, were her lifeline. She figured as long as she wasn't required to say any words that required her to roll her tongue, she would be perfectly fine.

She found the Goldfarb's apartment and knocked, softly at first, but then with increased urgency as her fears began to take hold. *Oh great,* she began thinking, *they forgot I'm supposed to be here and now I'll be left in the hall endlessly.* Never one to overreact, Elizabeth began formulating a plan during her attack on the door. To her embarrassment, the door opened and she was staring at the sweetest old man she had ever seen, Mr. Goldfarb. Her babbling kicked in and she began offering her apologizes, realizing that while she had begun devising "Plan B," she had continued her incessant knocking.

"Barux haba!" was all that Mr. Goldfarb offered as he stepped out of her way and motioned for her to enter his home. Although Beth wasn't quite sure what he was saying, she knew from the twinkle in his eyes that he was welcoming her. She nodded a simple response that she hoped said, *Thank-you for your kindness and thoughtfulness.* Taking two steps into the Goldfarb residence Beth was overcome by fatigue and hunger. She rolled her suitcase off to the side of the small foyer area and clasped her hands together. *Now what?* She said to herself.

Chapter Five

*Say not to your neighbor, "Go, and
come again, tomorrow I will give,"
when you can give at once.*
Proverbs 3:28

The aroma of chicken soup and gefilte fish filled the small, orderly Goldfarb apartment. If ever there was an image rendered in any of Beth's books about cozy rooms filled with just enough knick-knacks to say "home" but not too much to appear cluttered, this room was it. It had one loveseat sized couch that was a beautiful, muted blend of flowers on vines. The over-stuffed cushions begged you to recline and rest your weary frame. Beth was immediately taken by its size as it could easily fit two but would never fit three. In front of it sat two delicately embroidered footstools, one for each of the couch's occupants. The pattern on each footstool complimented the flowery couch with its subtle colors of rich, dark green, equally deep gold, and a reddish-burgundy that reminded Elizabeth of Luke's favorite cabernet wine.

On each side of the couch was an end table. While both were made of a cherry colored wood, one was round and the other square. The round end table had a few beautifully framed pictures of people smiling, celebrating birthdays, and enjoying the sites of Israel. The square table had its own shelf underneath the top glass portion. The bottom shelf was filled with magazines and a bowl of candy. Making a sort of "L" shape in the room was a chair next to the square shaped end table. Both the occupant sitting on one end of the couch and whomever might be enjoying the extra large chair would have shared the light from the large gold and ceramic lamp that sat upon the square end table, its fringed shade adding a certain elegance to the setting. The back of the couch was against a fairly large picture window which was covered in a sheer panel with heavier drapes pulled off to each side. The window was slightly opened and the thin, almost translucent drape covering it moved gently with the incoming breeze. Each soft billow seemed to let in a fragment of traffic noise from the street below. The view was ever so slightly obscured, allowing the Goldfarbs to enjoy seeing their city while keeping their city from seeing them.

Just as the back of the couch was against a window, the remaining part of the "L" shape of the furniture, the chair, was against a wall that must have been one of the two bedrooms in the apartment. Opposite the chair, at the other end of the couch, was a small, round dining table. It was the same cherry colored wood that went so well with the colors of the couch, footstools, and chair. The tiny kitchen was opposite the table where Mrs. Goldfarb could cook and glance across her neatly decorated room and enjoy both any company she might have or look out the window.

When Mrs. Goldfarb appeared she was wearing an apron that reminded Beth of her own grandmother's cooking attire. Beth fondly recalled how her grandmother kept an apron on hand and never, ever cooked without slipping it over her head and then tying it behind her waist which increased in size, just as Beth's was currently doing. Mrs. Goldfarb smiled at Beth and said, "Please, please, come in, sit down. Please!"

In life Beth came across many people who extended invitations with little or no real expectation that they should be accepted. Most certainly she did it too. Mrs. Goldfarb was not one of those people and Elizabeth happily accepted the gracious request to sit. It also helped that Mrs. Goldfarb clearly had some command of the English language as Beth was too tired to try her hand at piecing a sentence together. "Thank you," was Beth's simple reply as she followed both Mr. and Mrs. Goldfarb into their apartment. Mr. Goldfarb motioned towards the chair and Beth sat down, exhaustion creeping into her bones.

"So, how was your flight?" Mr. Goldfarb inquired.

Nodding her head to indicate her positive response, Beth said, "Good. Very good." She didn't know how much to say for fear of disrupting the delicate conversation that had begun. She would take her cue from the Goldfarbs and hope that they understood she was trying to be a gracious guest.

"We've made the trip several times." Mrs. Goldfarb offered. The "r" in the word trip sort of rolling elegantly off her tongue.

"Do you have relatives in the states or do you vacation there?" Beth wondered out loud.

"Bot, really." Mr. Goldfarb, dropping the 'h' from the word 'both,' joined the conversation. Mrs. Goldfarb had made a quick trip to the kitchen and was walking back with a tray of cheese, flat bread, a few pieces of smoked salmon, and quite a few black olives. The food looked delicious. Mr. Goldfarb went on to tell Beth about his brother who moved to New York many years ago and was a successful grocer. It was his only brother and that made visiting very important to both men. Mrs. Goldfarb, it turned out, also had a brother living in the United States. He, however, lived in California.

When they were younger, Mrs. Goldfarb confessed, they could take traveling across America and spending time with each brother for a week or so. Age, unfortunately, had taken that from them and their trips had to have a single goal in mind. Spring was when they spent time with Mr. Goldfarb's brother and fall was when they visited Mrs. Goldfarb's brother. Throughout their discourse, each taking a turn to add to the story of their trips, Beth could feel herself relaxing more than she had in years. Wrapped in the safe cocoon of the Goldfarb apartment, Beth could feel the stress evaporate. Between the wonderful aromas wafting from the kitchen to their beautiful use of the English language, Beth was enthralled.

"Mrs. Goldfarb, what smells so heavenly?" Beth inquired.

"Tsk. Tsk. Please, do not call me Mrs. Goldfarb! Please call me Ayala. And it is challah for today's Sabbath meal. We hope you will join us. We thought you would enjoy this light snack and would want to settle into your apartment across the hall, maybe take a small nap and then come back. Our children will be here tonight and they would love to make your acquaintance."

"Mrs. Goldfarb, I mean Ayala, I could not intrude on your family's Sabbath celebration!"

"You do not understand. For us to share our Sabbath dinner with you is a mitzvot." Ayala Goldfarb could see that this dear sweet American girl did not understand and went on to explain. "A mitzvot is a good deed and it would please God if we shared our Sabbath meal with a stranger in a strange land. We were once ourselves strangers in a strange land. Please, allow us to do a mitzvot that would be pleasing to God. Have Sabbath dinner with us."

Beth knew she could not deny Ayala this chance to do a 'mitzvot' and said, "Well, then, that sounds like a wonderful plan. If you will give me the keys, I will go across the hall and get myself settled, relax a bit, and then join you and your family later this afternoon."

"Perfect. This is good," was Meir Goldfarb's hearty reply.

Standing up, Beth realized how very weary she actually was as it didn't seem her legs had enough strength to walk her across the hall. "Toda," Beth said as she left.

Smiling, Meir and Ayala responded, "You're velcome." Beth loved the way their w's sounded like v's and their r's took on a life of their own. She walked across the hall, looked back as she turned the key, smiled at the wonderful angels that had come into her life, and opened the door. As she stepped over the threshold, Beth heard the Goldfarb's door close and then she closed and locked her own. She turned and looked into an apartment that was almost a mirror image of theirs, without the mouth-watering smells. Beth liked what she saw and rolled her suitcase down the narrow hall to the bedroom. First she peeked in on the room on her right, the room that shared a wall with the living room. It seemed to be set up as a guest bedroom with a twin bed, a desk and chair, a chest of drawers, and a small valet on which to hang clothes. It was a fairly small room but served its purpose. The second room that Beth looked into was the larger bedroom and the room that Beth would use. It had a queen size bed, a vanity chair placed at a small Queen Anne style dressing table, a larger chest of drawers than in the first room, and a taller, thin dresser.

Wheeling her suitcase off to the side, Beth pulled back the curtains. The window overlooked a picturesque garden and Beth was quite grateful. She had heard that the city streets, while enjoyable during the waking hours, could be a real nuisance while one tried to sleep. That was probably her only real priority when the traveler's agent was making inquiries for her. Beth insisted on a room that would allow her to actually sleep! Beth walked around opening the dresser drawers and was pleasantly surprised at the drawer liners that were in place. They had the soft sweet smell of lavender and Beth selected the three largest drawers to use during her stay. She knew if she wasn't careful, she would end up leaving half her belongings in Israel and decided to confine her use to these three drawers plus the drawer of the dressing table.

Once again a severe feeling of fatigue engulfed Beth and she decided to shower before she began to unpack. She laid her suitcase flat on the floor and unzipped it. She sifted through her neatly folded clothes to find her loungewear and toothbrush. She then left the room and went to the end of the hall where the bathroom was located. It actually ran the entire length of the second bedroom which accounted for her bedroom being a good five feet longer than the first one she looked into. It was a very nice size room with an interesting shower rod. The rod had two bars. One, on the inside, which held the shower curtain on its rings. The other, on the outside, had clips from which you could hang things to dry. Beth remembered being told that there was a washer in a closet in the bathroom and opened a door to see that it was indeed there.

The bathroom was spotless and Beth was quite pleased. She also saw a small bucket of cleaning items in the bathroom closet and, on a shelf, spotted some rags. On a higher shelf were three large white towels and two hand towels. There was no washcloth but Beth had never been a washcloth user. She opened a new box of soap and undressed. She put her clothes in a small hamper that was under the sink and turned on the water. Taking a shower anywhere other than home was always an adjustment and this was no different.

Her own shower had a forceful spray that Beth thoroughly enjoyed. It always seemed to wash the knots in her neck completely away. This shower was more like a mist and Beth wondered if she would actually be able to wash her hair. There didn't seem to be enough water pressure. She reached her hand in and within a minute the temperature felt right. She stepped in and felt a bit off balance. She looked around and steadied herself, knowing that the heat of the shower, combined with the exhaustion and time differences, was making her a bit lightheaded. She finished her shower and stepped out onto a thick cotton rug, dried herself, and put on her loungewear.

She stopped in front of her bedroom door deciding if she should succumb to her exhaustion or push herself a few more hours. Exhaustion won out and she turned into her bedroom. Pulling back the thin comforter, Beth noticed a robe hanging on the back of the door. It had a welcoming note indicating that it was a present from the apartment owners. Beth lifted it off the hook and laid it across the pillow. She didn't want her wet hair to ruin the pillow. Lying on her back, Beth placed her wet head on the robe, pulled a light sheet over her, and fell fast asleep.

Chapter Six

Trust in the Lord and do good that you may dwell in the land and live secure. Psalm 37:3

Luke was startled out of his daydream by the intercom. "Mr. Gantry, there is a call for you on line two. It's Mr. McFarland regarding this afternoon's meeting. Did you want to take the call?"

"Thanks Meghan. I'll take it." Luke had been waiting for this call for three days. He had offered McFarland quite a deal on the computer equipment that McFarland's company was interested in purchasing.

"Hell-o, John. How are you today?"

"Excellent, Luke. Thank you. I was hoping you and I could go over some preliminary data before our meeting this afternoon. I would like to leave with a contract signed. I assume you have no objections?"

Chuckling, Luke responded, "As long as there are no major hurdles, I believe we will have a long and productive relationship. I look forward to helping you meet all your computer needs and know that you will be more than pleased with our commitment to quality and service."

"Well, I have to admit that is why it has taken me a few days to get back to you. I wanted to make some phone calls before I signed over our hard earned money." Both men felt a great sense of relief at having come to an agreement. They were now moving into Luke's favorite part of being a business owner; becoming friends.

Luke's business ethics were a direct result of his father's teaching through example. Having arrived in the United States with only enough money to rent a small room, Luke's dad had worked long and hard to save enough money to send for his bride and their children. Eventually Luke's mother and older siblings moved to America to join Luke's father. By then he had established himself as "an American" and had started a small business as a tailor. He made beautiful suits and dresses and coats. Of course, as a youngster, Luke never appreciated his father's talent or the amount of time his dad gave to his work. Luke just took it for granted that everyone's father worked as hard as his did and, to this day, was dumbfounded by lazy men.

Luke was the last of Norma and Arthur's children. Luke was the baby of the family and, as such, was always very special, as babies of the family often are. Beth thought of Sammy and understood how the last child took a special place, representing the end of an era for the mother, so to speak. Luke was doted on more than any of the other Gantry children, a practice that never stopped. To this day Luke was clearly Norma's favorite.

After Luke finished his conversation with John McFarland, he hung up and returned to his thinking of Liz. What he had always taken for granted, long hours and numerous business trips, Liz had started to regret. It was as if she wanted all the trappings that accompanied his success without any of the sacrifices. He long ago stopped trying to explain to her that she couldn't have both. He felt like he was talking to a wall. Then, one day, her frustration with his work schedule stopped. At first he was delighted and felt that a real burden had been lifted off his shoulders. But it soon became apparent that her grumbling ceased because she was moving her life in a different direction. A direction that didn't include him. All of a sudden her complaining didn't seem all that bad and he began getting worried.

Whereas she used to limit her visits with her friends to the daytime, so as not to interfere with their family dinners, she was now getting together with her friends whenever it suited her. Luke hated to admit it, but she was becoming selfish and he didn't know what to do. He knew when she proposed taking this trip to Israel that there was really no stopping her. Although he had felt like he had been punched in the gut, he kept his reactions to himself. He wasn't sure what she was looking for from him but he was getting exhausted trying to figure it out. It was almost ironic, but he was looking forward to this reprieve from the emotional demands of their daily relationship.

No one in Luke's family had been divorced and he was seriously wondering if he was going to be the first. He felt almost numb as he contemplated such an idea. And, he told himself, if that was going to be the case, he was glad his father wasn't alive to see it.

Luke had to shake himself out of this depressing way to think and focus on putting the finishing touches on the contract. He was pleased that John had decided to pick up the warranty for the computer systems. Luke knew many businesses that made a great deal of money from warranties but his company wasn't one of them. He used the funds collected from these sales to provide on-going maintenance that seemed to keep long-term problems at bay.

Luke smiled as he thought of his dad encouraging his customers to pay a few cents more for finishing tape along the seams and hems of a garment. That was the warranty work that his father had provided. The clothes lasted longer and customers returned again and again, knowing that they were getting more than their money's worth when they had a suit or dress made by Arthur Gantry, tailor extraordinaire.

Chapter Seven

My help comes from the Lord, the
maker of heaven and earth.
Psalm 121:2

The urgent knocking at the door startled Beth from her sleep. At first she couldn't quite rouse herself and simply turned onto her side and pulled more covers around her neck. She was caught in between sleep and wake and preferred sleep. However, the knocking wouldn't stop and Beth shook the slumber from her brain. *Who is at the door?* She wondered. And then, as if a bolt of lightning ran through her, she sat straight upright. Stumbling, she made her way to the door.

The stranger at the door stared at Elizabeth. While Beth stood motionless, trying to get her bearings, the young woman smiled and Beth immediately saw the resemblance between her and Mrs. Goldfarb, Ayala. Beth knew that this woman who couldn't take her eyes off Beth's snarled mane must be Ayala's daughter. Beth raised her hands and made a meager attempt at calming her hair down but knew it was no use. Beth was blessed with beautiful, thick sandy blonde hair that had a mind of its own. Since Beth had fallen asleep with it wet, she knew it was, at that very moment, a tangled mess atop her head. She smiled sheepishly and said, "You must be Ayala's daughter. Please, come in. I'm sorry, I fell asleep. The exhaustion..."

Beth's sentence trailed off as the Goldfarb daughter simply said, "Please, please, do not worry. We know you are exhausted. We did not want you to sleep too much though, because your whole schedule will be off. We want you to come over and have a good Sabbath meal and then we will let you get back into bed. I believe my parents have plans for you tomorrow and you need to be well rested!"

"You are too kind," Beth paused, wanting to use her name but nothing coming to mind. She couldn't remember if the Goldfarb's had told her or not. She stood embarrassed, but only for a fleeting moment.

"My name is Miriam. And I am delighted to make your acquaintance, Beth. Now please, take your time, get dressed, and come across the hall. We are looking forward to sharing a meal with you." At that Miriam turned and crossed the hall. Beth closed her own door and reflected on her good fortune at having found such a warm and inviting family as her neighbors on this trip. Yes, God sure was watching out for her!

Making her way to the bathroom, Beth devised a plan to get herself in a presentable way that wouldn't take another hour. She couldn't make her gracious hosts wait on her account. She ran her hairbrush under the water and pulled it through her mop of hair. Using a blow dryer Beth stood in front of a mirror in an attempt to remove some of the volume that had erupted during her sleep. Beth watched her reflection, in quiet dismay, as her arms, one raised above her head holding the blow dryer and the other raised holding the brush, showed her age.

Of all the things that she couldn't get used to, it was the loose area of flesh and skin under her arms. There were less and less signs of age that she could cover up and she considered her flabby arms to be her Waterloo. She spent countless hours doing arms presses on the weight machines her sons had at home. Diligently, she walked the local track or rode her own exercise bike. But to what avail? Drying her hair she thought it was time to accept defeat and move into the next phase of life, toneless arms and all.

Putting down her brush, semi-satisfied with her clean up job, Beth looked at the clock. She knew she needed to call Luke but had been putting it off until she had a reason for it to be a short, painless conversation. Dinner with the Goldfarbs was the perfect excuse for an *'I'm here and fine. Please tell the kids I love them. I have to go'* contact with her husband. She picked up the phone and dialed. It was late-afternoon in Israel which meant it was around eight in the morning in Michigan. Luke should be at work and Beth dialed his direct office number.

One of their agreements, after counseling, had been that Luke put in a direct line so that Beth wouldn't always feel like a "client" or "customer" when she called. She adored Luke's secretary but often felt odd asking to speak to her husband. One time Meghan actually hesitated, not seeming sure if she should put Elizabeth's call through to Luke. That did it and Luke installed a private line the next day.

"Hey, my little world traveler!" were Luke's first words to Beth.

Taken off guard, Beth's heart filled with emotion for her husband. "Hi, honey. How are you?"

"Except for the hole in our morning where your presence was sorely missed, I'm great. The kids got off to school just fine. Sophia was more than helpful with Sammy and that made the morning better than I expected. She also threw in a load of wash on her way out. She said she'll put it in the dryer when she gets in from school. I don't think she's working this afternoon. I gave everyone a few extra dollars for lunch and asked each of them to call me when they got home from school. We should be fine so make sure you enjoy yourself. How was your flight?"

"Actually, everything went quite well. I did my best to sleep but ended up taking a nap just now. And, of all things, I've been invited to dinner by the neighbors. They are wonderful and are waiting for me so I want to get going." There was a slight hesitation as neither seemed to know what to say.

"Okay, then. I'm glad you are in good hands. I know you told me not to expect daily calls, but I do hope you will try to call a couple of times a week. I know it is difficult for you to say because you don't know what your trip will hold, but still, give it a try." Luke was doing his best to give Beth her space, as if Israel weren't far enough and she needed more.

"I will," was Beth's response. "Have a good day and give the kids a big hug and kiss for me. And tell Sophia how much it means to me that she is pitching in. It makes me feel like somehow, somewhere, you and I have done a good job, Luke."

"We love you," was Luke's safe reply.

Elizabeth also remained in neutral territory, "My love to everyone."

Opening her luggage, Beth decided to get a few things hung up before she headed to the Goldfarb apartment. She was already getting deliciously lost in the silence that surrounded her and felt as if she could, for the first time in ages, hear her own thoughts. There were no televisions on in the background, no kids arguing with each other, no one calling her name. If there was a still, small voice wanting to speak to her, she would finally be able to listen.

Beth knew that Sabbath began shortly before sundown and could feel the beauty of the occasion in the air. The sun was low in the sky and the weather could not have been more cooperative. She pulled on a light, long sleeved cotton jersey shirt and a pair of stretch denim-like pants. Both the shirt and pants were complementary tones of forest green, Beth's favorite color. The shirt had a bit of embroidery around the scoop neckline and sleeve cuffs. She stood, looking in the full length mirror attached to the back of the bedroom door and contemplated tucking in her shirt. She had a belt, so it wasn't that. She just was at that point where sucking in her stomach had lost its appeal.

It wasn't as if she were really overweight; there were only an extra ten or twelve pounds on her frame. It was just that they were all in her waist and bottom. Where she once could get by with one piece outfits and tucked in tops, she now bought clothes that hid her mid-section. She wasn't coping well with the onslaught of middle age. Thinking of her request for water on the plane and the entire idea of this trip, Beth decided to continue with her carefree wild streak. She tucked in her top, ruffled through her bag to find her belt and pulled on a pair of cream colored socks. She grabbed her brown shoes and went into the living room. Sitting on a dining chair, she pulled on her shoes and grabbed the keys off the counter. She surveyed the room, nodded in approval, and headed towards the door. Letting herself out, her back still to the Goldfarb's apartment, she could smell all the wonderful Sabbath aromas as they filled the hallway. Smiling, she walked over to Meir and Ayala's and knocked.

"Shabbat Shalom!" Welcomed Meir. "Please, come in," he motioned for Beth to move into their inviting home and join his family.

Beth awkwardly realized that she had nothing to offer her host or hostess and did her best not to begin apologizing. "Shabbat Shalom," she responded. And, walking into the room exchanged greetings with the young woman who had so kindly roused Beth from her sleep. Sitting next to Miriam on the couch was a young man who looked strikingly like Meir. Beth often marveled at how she could see resemblances in other families but never in her own. People always told her how her children looked like Luke or looked like herself, but she never saw it. She smiled at the young man as he introduced himself.

"Shabbat Shalom. I am David Goldfarb, Meir and Ayala's son. Welcome to Israel."

Both Goldfarb children looked to be in their twenties but it was difficult to tell. Beth was never good at telling ages and had long given up. More likely they were in their thirties, based on the Meir and Ayala's ages who looked to be in their sixties. "Thank you so much. I am delighted to be here and cannot believe my good fortune at having met your parents. They are wonderful and kind people."

David smiled knowingly, "I've long ago learned that Adonai's hand is in all things and am not surprised that you are under the care of my parents. Yes, they are wonderful and kind people."

Taking the pre-offered chair that she had sat in that afternoon, Beth made herself comfortable. Meir had pulled up one of the dining chairs and was talking animatedly with his children. There seemed to be a tense moment or two and then they all remembered that they had a guest. Ayala kept busy in the kitchen and Elizabeth simply succumbed to the atmosphere of food and family. How ironic that she would find herself so at ease in the home of strangers, albeit warm and friendly ones. What was drawing her in so fully, so completely?

"Could everyone please come to the table? I would like to begin our Sabbath meal." Everyone stood up at Ayala's request and made the few necessary steps towards their dinner seats. Meir brought with him the chair he had been using and placed it at the beautifully set table. Either Ayala had gone all out for her visitor or the Goldfarbs celebrated the weekly Sabbath to the degree that Elizabeth celebrated Christmas and Easter. What appeared to be the best china, bone colored with a silver trim, was set upon a splendid lace tablecloth, obviously hand sewn with great love. Water goblets and wine glasses caught the light from the hanging chandelier. The silverware had long handles with what looked like intricately carved ribbons on the end of each piece. Linen napkins, the same color as the plates, completed each place setting. The table was full of large and small platters filled with aromatic dishes and a small tureen of chicken soup.

Beth stood behind a chair indicating her question of appropriateness and was given a nod from Ayala. It was subtle and Beth appreciated Ayala's comfortable ways. Meir, Miriam, and David each stood behind a chair as well and Beth could see that this was the correct stance for the beginning of the meal. Ayala walked back into the kitchen to get two magnificent candle holders. Each was about the height of the tall water goblets with the candle extending about six inches above. The candle holders were a burnished gold about two inches in diameter. They were fairly plain except for the middle where there was a thick band of gold vines winding their way around each stem. That same band was repeated at the base of the candle holders.

Covering her head in what looked like a lace shawl, Ayala waited while Miriam offered the same head covering to Elizabeth. Taking her cue from Miriam, Beth gently placed the lace upon her head and let it drip down onto the tops of her shoulders. She was transformed as she watched Meir and David put on their own head coverings, yarmulkes. Moving the candle sticks so that they were directly in front of her place setting, Ayala took out a packet of matches and lit the candles. She then blew out the small flame of the match and placed it on the very edge of her plate. She bowed her head down, closed her eyes, and began making a circular motion above the flames. Her open arms reached out as if she were going to hug someone and then circled back in, towards her chest. She began praying, "Barukh atah Adonai, Eloheinu melekh ha olom, ah sher keed shahnu be meetzvotav, vit zee vahnu, li had leek neir shel Shabbat." Ayala repeated this three times and with each time made the same outward and inward circular motions with her hands.

Meir then blessed the wine. "Barukh atah Adonai, Elohaynu, melekh ha-olam, borei p'riy ha-gafen."

Beth was overcome with emotion and hoped she wouldn't embarrass herself and begin crying. Menopause was the gift that kept on giving.

Ayala, once again showing her instinctive ability to read other people, looked at Elizabeth and began explaining the Sabbath celebration.

"First, let me begin by sharing with you the meanings of the words of our prayers. When I light the candles I am saying, 'Blessed are You, oh God, our Lord, King of all creation whose commandments make us holy and who commands us to light the candles of Sabbath.' When Meir blesses the wine he is saying, 'Blessed are You, Lord, our God, king of the universe who creates the fruit of the vine.'"

Ayala was serving soup along with her explanation and Beth was agreeing to both. As Beth began enjoying the delicious soup, Ayala continued the Sabbath lesson with Elizabeth intently listening. Meir would add comments here and there to the delight of everyone, even Ayala. Miriam and David clearly enjoyed their parents' moment in the spotlight and sat back for the lesson as well. All were transformed by the significance of the Sabbath as a call to remember and honor the Lord's day.

"Emma, I am embarrassed to ask . . . but I forgot why we light two candles," caught up in the moment Miriam was as childlike as Elizabeth as she listened to her mother and father. Ayala looked to Meir, obviously giving him permission to explain this while Ayala enjoyed her own soup. Meir's bowl was empty and it seemed like a fair trade.

Before Meir began, Ayala turned to Beth and said, "My daughter calls me 'emma' which means 'mother' and calls Meir 'abba' which means 'father'." Beth's spoon stopped halfway to her mouth as she realized that Jesus called His father, Abba. Abba! Beth loved the sound of it: Abba.

Meir then began telling his audience that two candles are lit because the Ten Commandments appear twice in the Torah. First, they are in Exodus, which was when they were actually given to Moses. They appear the second time in Deuteronomy, just prior to Moses' death, when he is again sharing them with his people. The Jewish people note that there is a significant difference in these two events. In the first instance, in Exodus, the command is to 'remember the Sabbath day and keep it holy' while the second instance, in Deuteronomy, the command changes and the people are told to "guard" the Sabbath and keep it holy. So the two candles signify the two different words used to express the commands regarding the Sabbath. One is to remember, zachor, and the other is to guard, shamor.

While Meir had explained the difference between zachor and shamor, Ayala had cleared away the soup dishes and was serving succulent chicken, vegetables, and blessed company. Beth enjoyed the dinner conversation and could easily see how very close the Goldfarbs were with one another. Eventually the evening came to an end with a cup of thick, rich coffee and a serving of compote, a mouth watering mixture of ripe fruit served in a pretty crystal bowl.

Plans were finalized to attend synagogue the next morning as Beth agreed to spend the Sabbath day with the Goldfarbs. Meir explained to Beth that the Sabbath day was one of visiting, discussing Torah, and praying. Beth was intrigued and looked forward to the day.

Getting up to leave, Elizabeth was embraced, one by one, by the Goldfarb clan. Miriam walked her to the small foyer and watched as Beth unlocked her own apartment door and entered. Beth heard Miriam close the Goldfarb door only after Beth's own latch had been secured.

Yes, Beth thought, *David is right. Adonai's hand is most definitely in this newfound relationship.*

Chapter Eight

As Mountains surround Jerusalem,
the Lord surrounds his people both
now and forever. Psalm 125:2

Elizabeth's first day in Israel had been a huge success. Everything that she had prayed for seemed to have materialized. When Beth planned the trip her interest was in experiencing the fabric of everyday life in the Promised Land, not in the removed experience of a tourist or vacationer. Elizabeth wanted to know, up close and personal, what it was like to live as a "chosen one." It was a phrase that she had both envied and feared during her many bible study groups. Having taught middle school for the better part of a dozen years, Beth knew the perks that came from being a "chosen" one in a school setting. Usually they were the athletes or the kids who behaved and excelled in all they did. Their accomplishments stacked up like pancakes at the local IHOP restaurant. They were "chosen" and there wasn't anything that could stand in their way.

The Jews, however, didn't have that same experience. Beth was particularly absorbed in the story of Judge Deborah when it occurred to her the tremendous burden that came with that precious title. Her heart skipped a beat reading about Jael and Judge Deborah following God's call on their lives and defeating the Canaanites. Yes, it was a great burden to be God's chosen people with as many punishments as there were rewards. This was very unlike anything that the typical "chosen" students at school had ever experienced. You couldn't help but pause at the implications.

Beth washed her face, brushed her teeth, and put her clothes on the back of the vanity chair. She pulled on her lounge pants and a long sleeved t-shirt. Her final effort of the day was made in throwing her socks in the hamper and pulling on a pair of fresh white cotton new ones.

Ready for bed, Beth walked right past the bedroom and into the living room of what was to be her home for the next two weeks. She saw a few magazines and newspapers on a small end table that was located between two very large chairs and decided to read for a few minutes before settling in for the night. The coffee had a bit more power than her fatigue and she knew better than to climb in bed only to toss and turn. She clicked on the floor lamp next to one of the chairs and settled into the firm seat. It had a reclining feature and she pushed a button that brought out the hidden footrest.

Groaning, she remembered that she needed her glasses and pushed the footstool back under so that she could get out of the chair. Walking over to the counter on which she had placed her tote bag, she searched for her glasses. Finding them, she shuffled back to the chair, relieved to feel a slow sense of sleep settling into her mind and body.

Picking up the magazine, Beth was pleasantly surprised to see that it was a Christian edition of the Jerusalem Post. Wondering who could have been so thoughtful to leave this paper for her enjoyment, she read through the table of contents. The paper was published by the Jerusalem Post, which was an English paper. This particular edition included an interview with a well known Christian author, speaker, and advocate of Israel. It also held articles touting the beauty of Galilee among other things. No longer than fifty pages, the magazine was sure to become Beth's favorite reading material over the next few days. She knew she would read it cover to cover and began with the "News in Brief" articles.

Before she finished the fifth small summary, Beth was close to falling asleep. Knowing her back would need a mattress and not a chair, she forced herself to get up and get into bed. Barely getting through her nighttime devotions of gratitude and praise, she was fast asleep.

Chapter Nine

*The Lord will guard your coming and
going both now and forever.
Psalm 121:8*

Never one to need an alarm, Beth was up early
on her first morning in Israel. She was looking
forward to attending synagogue with the Goldfarbs,
while not really knowing what to expect. While
Beth's conversations with God and her devotional
time remained consistent, her own church attendance
was sporadic at best. For the past few years she felt
a longing and an inability to fill a void that seemed to
be growing more cavernous with each passing day.
Elizabeth felt that any and all help the Lord was
willing to throw her way would be greatly
appreciated.

Having been assured by Ayala that it would be
perfectly acceptable to "work" on the Sabbath, Beth
felt somewhat relieved that she wouldn't be expected
to follow Jewish customs and practices completely.
Although she would have, out of respect to her
wonderful hosts, she was glad that exceptions would
be made for her.

The Goldfarbs, however, would maintain their
strict observance of the Sabbath which meant no
cooking or any other activities that constituted work.
Beth, on the other hand, would have her cake and eat
it too. She would have the freedom to do as she
pleased, but would also enjoy whatever the day would
hold with the friends and neighbors of Meir and
Ayala. Beth thought of the Goldfarb children and felt
a bit of a pull at her heart. *How funny*, thought Beth,
to call adults "children." Beth was beginning to feel

an ache for her own children. She silently asked God to watch out for them and to let them feel her love through the time and space that separated them.

Having given the matter over to God, Elizabeth moved around the apartment feeling a great sense of peace. All was right with the world as she walked into the kitchen area to put on a pot of coffee. Off the kitchen was a small balcony that had an inviting wicker table flanked by two wicker chairs. The cushions looked worn but clean and Beth decided it would be the perfect place for a cup of coffee and more reading of the magazine. The coffee pot was clean and located on the counter right below the cupboard that held the coffee grounds, sugar, coffee cream, and cups. Spoons were in a drawer to the right with the other utensils. Filling the coffee pot with water Beth found herself humming. Although she would have been hard pressed to identify the tune, she was nonetheless humming!

Looking at the coffee choices, she was once again delighted to see the thoughtfulness that went into her comfort. Along with a couple of different blends that would be in keeping with coffee she would find in the states, there were two intriguing coffees that were apparently made in Israel. Opening one of the blue and red foil bags, Beth was greeted by wonderfully aromatic coffee. Luke, being the real coffee lover in their house, came quickly to mind. She knew he would love to share a freshly brewed cup of coffee with her on the terrace and wondered how he and the kids were doing.

Settling on the freshly ground coffee from Israel that smelled like vanilla and cinnamon, Elizabeth clicked the coffee pot on and decided to splash some water on her face before heading outside. She also remembered to pick up her reading glasses.

Stepping into her slippers, Beth made her way back to the kitchen just as the coffee finished brewing. The fragrance filled the kitchen. Beth liked the large cups that she found in the cupboard and poured herself a steaming cup of coffee. Tucking the newspaper under her arm and slipping her reading glasses into her pocket, Beth opened the terrace door. It was a sliding glass door that moved easily on the tracks.

The morning was exquisite and Beth couldn't get over her continued good fortune. The temperature was comfortable, maybe in the mid-sixties. Beth settled into one of the wicker chairs and looked out at the slumbering city. She decided that this would be her spot for morning devotions and raised her cup to Adonai. *Shalom, Abba,* she said to her Creator and Lord. *Shalom. May this day give you honor and glory through the words and actions of all your people. May you continue to show us love, kindness, and mercy. Please accept my gratitude for the Goldfarbs and I ask that you bless them. I raise my own family to you, knowing that they are as precious to you as they are to me. Maybe even more so!*

Finishing her morning prayers, Beth picked up the newspaper and put on her reading glasses. They sat just enough down her nose to allow her to look over them at the emerging pedestrians and drivers below. Enjoying her coffee, Beth read through three complete articles before she realized that time was truly flying by and that she had promised to join the Goldfarbs for the Sabbath.

Gathering up her empty coffee cup, the newspaper, and her reading glasses, Beth went inside to shower and prepare for the day ahead. Whatever sleepiness was left after Beth's coffee was washed away in the warm shower. Elizabeth spent extra time with the conditioner, hoping to show the Goldfarbs that if nothing else, she could get her hair under control. Drying her hair Beth found herself humming again and made a note of this interesting development in her personality.

The weather looked to be a match of yesterday's and Beth decided upon a long skirt made of cotton jersey material that had just enough fabric to give her comfortable movement without being too flowing or dressy. The top Beth selected was also a taupe cotton jersey that pulled over her head and had two pretty pearl buttons at the neck. The entire wardrobe she brought to Israel was easy, ready to wear material and pieces.

She had found the stretch denim-like pants that she wore yesterday to be her best friend and had purchased them in every color. She then went around the store, carrying nine pairs of pants and matching tops. Her purpose was to attain a well groomed appearance while maintaining comfort throughout her trip. She felt she had been successful and now looked at her closet filled with drab, dull outfits, each looking less appealing than the last. *What were you thinking?* She asked to herself as she walked across the hall to the Goldfarb apartment. Within a few seconds Beth was tapping at the Goldfarb door. "Good morning!" Miriam said as she greeted Beth, "Shabbat Shalom."

"Shabbat Shalom," Beth comfortably responded to Miriam and marveled at how easily she had taken to the family. Usually Beth was quite reticent about new acquaintances but with the Goldfarbs had felt as if she had known them for ages.

"Emma and abba will be ready in a moment. David is just coming up the walk, I saw him out the window. We'll walk over to our synagogue on King George Street and then we'll walk to the homes of some friends who live a few streets over from there."

"Well, we have the perfect weather for it. Do you always attend synagogue together?"

"Yes, it has always been the one thing that emma and abba have insisted upon and now, well, we wouldn't have it any other way."

Beth felt a twinge of guilt hearing Miriam talk of the parental expectations of worshipping together. Beth had become lax, as had Luke, and their children were surely suffering because of it. She made a mental promise to address this issue when she returned home.

"Shabbat Shalom!" Ayala pulled Beth towards her for a hug and commented on Beth's "smart" outfit. Beth felt a bit better about her clothes. Maybe she was, as usual, being too hard on herself. She noticed that Ayala had a small, lace head covering. Ayala, never one to be caught unaware, noticed Beth's eyes take in the head covering. "We cover our head out of respect for Adonai. I have extras, would you like one?"

"I would," Beth heard herself saying. "That would be very generous of you. Would it be okay? Being that I am not Jewish?"

"Of course it would be okay! How could our Lord, blessed be His holy name, not love that you are honoring Him in such a way?" Ayala always had a way of saying things that made Beth feel the extent of God's agape love.

"Good morning, good morning, Bethula!" Meir had already turned Beth's name into a term of endearment and Beth was honored.

"Good morning, Meir. Shabbat Shalom."

Just as Beth was saying this to Meir, David walked in and greeted everyone. "Well, it looks like we are ready to go. Shall we?"

Walking down the stairs and out onto the street Beth felt as if she were part of a hypnotic crowd, people everywhere were moving in peaceful silence towards a predetermined destination. There were young and old, men and women, families and individuals. It was an amazing experience and Beth simply walked in the silence, once again feeling a great sense of gratitude and asking the Lord to prepare her heart for worship. They arrived a few minutes before the nine o'clock service was to begin. Beth used the time to sit in her seat and take in her surroundings. The shul, another word that David used when talking about the synagogue, was quite impressive.

It was larger than Beth expected and quite modern looking. *What were you thinking*, she said to herself, *Herod's Temple?* Getting past her disappointment, Beth walked in with the dozens of other people who had taken the same route. She followed the Goldfarbs to cushioned, fairly luxuriant chairs and settled in. Looking around she noticed a magnificent scroll that took her breath away. *Now this*, she thought, *was what I was hoping for!*

The synagogue had no paintings, no statues, but was beautiful nonetheless. Beth was trying to make mental notes of things she would later ask Meir, Ayala, David, or Miriam. To her delight, David began giving her a lesson in the layout of the building. "The east wall is where the ark is kept. It is behind that elaborately decorated curtain and it is why we are facing east. It is the center of our worship and our focus during our time here."

Beth nodded to show David her appreciation of the information he was sharing. It was her hope that he would feel free to continue and he did. "Above the ark is a lamp called *'ner tamid'* which shows that God is always there. It literally means 'eternal light' and comes from the middle candle of the first menorah that did not stop burning. You will see when the curtain is drawn back that the Torah is also covered in a beautifully decorated velvet wrap. The Torah is part of what you call 'The Old Testament.' It is actually the first five books of it and everything we do revolves around our love of these words, inspired by God, and our obedience to them." It looked as though the service was about to start and David's silent attention went towards the ark.

Beth began thinking of Christ, himself a Jew, studying Torah. She knew this to be the case as He had so often used these words to reveal Himself as the fulfillment of them to God's people. It was an amazing understanding for Beth as she, too, concentrated on the ark.

The service was longer than Beth had anticipated, close to three hours total, and yet she enjoyed it immensely. Walking towards a friend's home where they would enjoy an afternoon of visiting and eating, David picked up where he had left off. "The first part of the service was the blessings and hymns. Their purpose is to focus our minds and heart on the everlasting glory of our Creator. We begin by saying the 'Birchot Ha-Shachar' which are the morning blessings. These blessings make us aware of the incredible nature in every single thing we do and everything around us. Saying these blessings bring to mind the miracle in even the smallest acts, like waking up and brushing our hair."

Beth was nodding as were Miriam, Meir, and Ayala. It was as if they were all thinking the same thing, *Who doesn't need to be reminded that every single part of our daily lives is an opportunity to praise God!*

David continued explaining the service. "The 'Baruch She'amar' is my favorite. We say, '*Baruch she'amar v'haya ha-olam Baruch she'amar' baruch Hu Baruch oseh, oseh v'reisheet Baruch omer v'oseh'* which means, 'Praised be the One who spoke and the world came to be. Praised be the Source of Creation. Praised be the One who spoke and the world came to be. Praised be God.' We follow this with the 'Ashrei,' which is our way to tell our God how we will exalt Him at all times. It is really quite beautiful, quite poetic, and very humbling to know that we serve a God who loves us so very much. It comes from one of King David's Psalms that says, 'Blessed are those who dwell in Your house." David continued explaining the service and Beth both heard and felt her stomach rumbling. She was hungrier than she had been in ages.

Miriam was asking David a question about the reading and studying of the Torah during service. All Beth caught was a portion of David's response, "Well, that is why, before we study it we say, '*Barchu et Adonai ha-m'vorach Ba-ruch Adonai ha-m'vorach l'olam va-ed Baruch Adonai ha-m'vorach l'olam va-ed Baruch ata Adonai, Eloheynu melech ha-olam asher bachar banu mi-kol ha-amim v'natan lanu et torato Baruch ata Adonai, noteyn ha-torah.*' which means, 'Blessed are You - the Lord our God, King of the Universe, who has chosen us from all peoples and has given us His Torah. Blessed are You - the Lord, Giver of the Torah.'

This is also why, when are finished reading from the Torah we say, '*Baruch ata Adonai, Eloheynu melech ha-olam. Asher natan lanu torat emet, v'cha-yey olam nata b'tocheynu, baruch atah Adonai noteyn ha-torah.*' Which means, 'Blessed are You - the Lord our God, King of the universe, who has given us the Torah of truth, and has planted everlasting life in our midst. Blessed are You - the Lord, Giver of the Torah.'"

"David, would it be possible for you to write down the English translations for me to keep? I find those words incredibly beautiful." Beth knew she wanted to say them before and after her own time in Scripture and then added, "Actually, is there a way to write in English, the Hebrew words?"

"There sure is and I would be glad to do that for you!"

They were now at the front door of an apartment building that looked larger than the one Beth was staying in; this one appeared to have six or seven stories and was a bit newer. Meir buzzed for the occupants of apartment D9, The Cohanes. Within a few seconds the buzzer sounded to release the lock and Meir held the door for everyone to get inside. Although the walk had been invigorating, none felt a need for the elevator. Beth was guessing that they would all sleep quite soundly tonight as they headed towards the stairs.

Arriving at the Cohane apartment, they were greeted by delicious aromas wafting into the hall as an elderly gentlemen held the door open for their welcome. Meir commented to Ayala, "Ben makes the best cholent! My mouth is already watering."

"I'm telling you," Ayala responded, "It is his butcher. I have been trying to get you to go to Ben's butcher for years now. Believe me, that cut of meat he gives Ben is so much better than what we get."

"Maybe you are right, Ayala. Next week, it's to Ben's butcher we will go!"

"Shabbat Shalom, Meir, Ayala, David, Miriam. Welcome. Welcome. How is everyone? And who is this? Is this the special sheyne meydele you told us about?" Beth smiled at Ben's question, getting a real kick out being called 'sheyne meydele' which Beth now knew meant 'pretty or beautiful girl.' Beth giggled like a teenager and smiled at Ben Cohane.

Ayala made the introductions and Ben ushered the small group into his charming home. Like the Goldfarbs', the Cohane's home was small and yet each piece of furniture was lovingly arranged and selected to ensure the comfort of any guests. Beth agreed with Meir that Ben probably made the best cholent ever. Of course the only thing she could base this on was the smell. And since she had never smelled cholent before, she was making a big presumption. However, her stomach seemed to be in agreement as it rumbled for some of the savory food whose delicious smells permeated the air.

Cholent, it turned out, was a slow cooking stew made with typical stew ingredients: beef and vegetables. It was a Sabbath standard because it could be put into an oven and cooked at a low temperature throughout the Sabbath night, thus supplying a meal for a household and any guests, without anyone having to work. The entire experience fascinated Beth as she enjoyed the questions and Torah study that ensued.

Beth had asked David to share more information about the morning service and he did so obligingly. He told Beth that the reason the Torah scroll is walked around the synagogue when it is taken from the ark, as well as when it is returned to the ark, is to show the great love and reverence that the congregants have for its teachings. David told his small audience that in many synagogues the people will even kiss the scroll to show their immense love for God's word. David was smiling at Meir as he said this last statement, and Beth knew that Meir must be one of those men who loved God's word so very much that he kissed the scroll. "Abba, what else can we share with our curious visitor?"

Meir joined the conversation by explaining that the reason the cover of the ark is so ornamental is in its purpose, which is to remind the people of the elaborate garbs of the priests from the temple days. Beth loved the symbolism and deep faith the Jews had in Adonai. She learned that those members of the congregation who had lost a loved one said the last prayer of the service, in silence. It is called the 'Mourner's Kaddish.' What Beth found so revelatory about the Kaddish was in its declaration that love and family are not separated by death.

The peaceful day continued with Meir and Ben playing a few games of chess while David spent some time reading through a study book on the Torah. The women, including Ben's wife Hannah, took a walk through the gardens in the back of the apartment complex. The day was perfect in every aspect, from the food to the company to the weather. Beth hadn't felt such tranquility in a long time and as they said their good-byes, she felt herself overcome with emotion towards yet another warm and generous family.

The walk back to their own apartment complex was a quiet one, each of them lost in his or her thoughts. As they approached the building, Miriam spoke up. "Well, I am going to head home, as is

David. I hope you have enjoyed your Sabbath in our country and that you will let us take you to the marketplace tomorrow. I'm sure you would enjoy having some time in your own apartment right now, unless of course there is anything you might need."

"Miriam, I couldn't ask for one more thing from you or David or your parents. Yes, I would love to visit the market tomorrow and would also be quite happy to spend a bit of time tonight lounging around the apartment, maybe doing a bit more reading. I have had the most perfect day today and feel that God couldn't bless me anymore!"

"Then it's settled," said Ayala. "We'll call it a day and will see you tomorrow when you wake up. Don't set an alarm or force any plans on yourself. We'll just take the day as it comes, whatever God gives us, we will embrace."

They all hugged as David and Miriam parted. David would drive Miriam to her apartment on his way home. Miriam lived about fifteen minutes from the Goldfarbs and David another five. It made their gatherings quite easy to maintain. Beth found herself hoping that her children would, one day, choose to live near her. She liked the idea of them being out from underfoot and yet close enough to see frequently! Although it was more than likely that Sophia would be living in New York where she could pursue her love of finance.

Beth knew Luke, too, hoped the kids would remain close but that Luke was more pragmatic, realizing that the children would go wherever their careers took them, just as he already accepted Sophia's move to the east coast.

Beth, Meir, and Ayala took the elevator up to their floor and each turned towards their own door,

"See you tomorrow. And again, thank you so much for such a beautiful day."

"You are welcome, Bethula. We'll see you tomorrow."

Chapter Ten

*He who finds a wife finds happiness; it
is a favor he received from the Lord.*
Proverbs 18:22

Luke was missing Liz more than he imagined
and it was only two days into her trip. When she had
first shared her plans, he had secretly welcomed the
idea of a break. But now two weeks lingered ahead of
him like a root canal staring at him from an
appointment book. *What had I been thinking to agree
to this?*

The boys had asked to have dinner at a
restaurant this evening and Luke had agreed.
Sophia was also available and that made the evening
extra special. She had become so busy with her
school work and job at the library that Luke felt as if
he never saw his daughter anymore.

The prospect of spending time with the kids
made Luke aware of the clock, something he often
ignored. It felt good to have responsibility outside of
work and Luke wondered where the boys might want
to eat. Sophia, like Luke, could eat just about
anywhere. Beth often said that Luke and Sophia had
stomachs made of steel while she and the boys had
less forgiving digestive systems.

He looked forward to having a nice dinner with
his children and hoped that there would be no rough
spots. Luke had become a bit weary from the battles
both he and Liz had so often had with their oldest
son, Michael.

Now with Michael in college, the family
dynamics had changed drastically. Michael, all of a

sudden, became interested in Luke's opinion about things and called home at least twice a week. Ironically, both Luke and Liz had assumed that they would be the ones chasing after a bone thrown by Mike now and again. Instead, Michael often called to find neither of his parents at home. Clearly they were enjoying the freedom from the scrimmages and had gotten on with their own lives. Much to Michael's dismay.

Luke recently heard Sophia talking with Michael on the phone and felt a twinge of relief that they had become friends after all. Both he and Beth had often worried if their children were ever going to get along.

Luke, who usually spent a good part of Saturday at work, finished early. He asked Meghan to cancel his latest appointment and headed home. Taking the boys and Sophia out to an early dinner, and maybe catching a movie, was starting to become a desirable prospect for Luke. The thought of spending quality time with the kids kept a smile on Luke's face all the way home.

Chapter Eleven

*How good it is, how pleasant, where the
people dwell as one!
Psalm 133:1*

Just as Ayala had instructed, Beth enjoyed a leisurely, quiet morning. She read a few more sections of the newspaper while she drank her coffee on the porch. The weather was a little cooler than the previous day and there was a bit of overcast to the sky. But that didn't put a damper on Beth's enthusiasm for a new day that held great promise.

Miriam had said that they were going to go to the "shuk," which was an outdoor marketplace. Beth eagerly anticipated the entire experience, knowing that the Goldfarbs would again ensure that her day was filled with the true essence of life in Israel.

Dressed in a pair of her casual pants, a long sleeve shirt, and grabbing a sweater, Beth headed over to the Goldfarbs. Tapping lightly on the door, she trusted that her timing was fine because Ayala said there would be no formal plans for the day.

"Shalom, Miriam. How are you today? You look wonderful!" Beth couldn't decide if she was seeing Miriam with different eyes because she now knew the beauty of Miriam's heart or if she had been so caught up in her own thoughts these past two days that she hadn't noticed Miriam's true physical beauty. Either way, Beth admired Miriam's strong cheekbones and large, almond eyes covered in lashes thicker than any Elizabeth had ever seen. Miriam's hair was a bit longer than shoulder length but cut in a way that its volume enhanced her face instead of being a distraction.

"Thank-you, you are kind. Please come in and share in our good news. We just found out that David has decided to accept a position in a rabbinic training program. This is something that he has been praying about for the past year. He will be a wonderful rabbi and we are all so very proud of him! Maybe the Lord used your conversation with him yesterday about synagogue and services to help him hear his heart on the matter." Miriam was almost bursting at the seams with pride and enthusiasm.

Beth felt quite honored that Miriam would even make such a suggestion that she could have had even a small part in such a wonderful event. Did the Lord use her to help David read his heart on this matter? The idea that such a thing could really happen, and that God could actually use people to help one another in such a significant way greatly affected her.

Beth couldn't help but get caught up in the moment and hugged Miriam. "Mazel-tov! What wonderful news!"

Just then David walked into the room flanked by Meir and Ayala. Even though Miriam had just invited Beth to join their celebration, Beth felt as if she were intruding on a very personal moment in their home. She was just about to beg off when Ayala rushed over to her and hugged her as if she had always been in their family. "Did you hear the most blessed news? My son, David, has decided to become a rabbi!"

"Yes, Miriam was just sharing that with me. Mazel-tov! It *is* wonderful news. Congratulations to you, Ayala. I know this is a very special time for you. Maybe you would prefer we shop another day? I don't want to intrude."

"Nonsense! This is the perfect day for you to spend with our family. It is a day of joy and celebration and God, blessed be His holy name, intends for you to share it with us. Did you have any breakfast yet?"

"No, actually I didn't. I enjoyed a couple of cups of coffee and read a magazine. I've become a lazy bum!"

Ayala laughed with Beth and said, "Good. We are planning to eat at the market today. We will get going before the crowds start and take all the fresh fish and fruit. Come, let's go then."

All five adults entered an empty elevator for a day of, as Ayala said, joy and celebration. Beth quietly thanked God for allowing her to be part of this event.

The Goldfarbs were divided in regards to which mode of transportation to initiate Elizabeth. Miriam and David felt that the train was most efficient and represented the best of their country's capabilities. Meir and Ayala, however, felt that walking was how God intended everyone to get around and insisted they all enjoy the beauty of the day and the hustle and bustle of the vibrant city life. The cooler temperatures added to the appeal of a leisurely stroll through the marketplace.

As they walked Beth asked questions about David's decision to become a rabbi and what would follow. He explained that there were still a few years between him and his goal but that it would be quite rewarding. Ayala confirmed that David had always been "a people person" and that the rabbinic lifestyle would suit him well.

Miriam, for the most part, remained silent but was beaming with pride. Beth wondered what her own children would grow up to be: a doctor, an engineer, a teacher, a priest. Would they get married? Would they want children? Would they move far away from her?

As usual, Beth exhausted herself with her meandering thoughts. If she could just learn to release them as quickly as they entered her mind, she could maintain her sanity. Unfortunately, once they made their appearance known, Beth owned them, tended to them, and nurtured them so that they could become full and complete burdens with a life of their own. This, of course, meant that the rest of the day Beth would deal with fleeting thoughts of her children's careers and marriages. She would do her best to ignore their trespassing, but experience taught her that would be futile. Resigned to this fact, Beth rejoined the Goldfarb conversation as best she could.

"No, let's stop and get something to eat before we shop," Meir was saying, apparently to someone's suggestion.

David, maybe practicing his mediating skills for his life as a rabbi said, "Why don't we compromise. There is a wonderful café about two blocks into the marketplace. We'll pass a few vendors along the way and can enjoy viewing their merchandise but won't pass our favorite vendors. That way we won't have packages to carry or watch while we eat."

Everyone seemed agreeable to this solution and Beth nodded, just to give the appearance that she had been listening the whole time. As they continued to walk Beth took in all the sights and sounds of the city. Cars and drivers were competing with one another both for right-of-way and in an attempt to out-scream each other. Although there didn't seem to be any real friction behind the escalating voices, Beth was glad that they were safe on the sidewalk.

Until, of course, Miriam quietly mentioned the number of pedestrian fatalities in the past year. Beth was shocked but as she watched the activities on the street, she felt she could understand. She became a bit more vigilant in paying attention to her proximity to the curb while listening to David and Meir discuss the benefits of fresh air. Meir obviously wanted David to be in agreement that walking had been their best alternative. David wholeheartedly agreed with his father and Elizabeth could see the makings of a special rabbi right before her very eyes.

"Here we go!" announced Miriam. Standing in front of a small café that Beth would have bet only existed in quaint books and stories, Miriam and Ayala made the decision to take the table closest to the potted palm tree. This gave way to merits of Israel's "Plant a Tree" program, all of which appeared to be positive.

Seated, everyone looked over at the small board that declared the morning specials. Having had enough coffee in the apartment, and not wanting to have to hunt down a restroom because of her ever-needy bladder, Beth declined any beverage. She would have no issue having to find a restroom for someone else but preferred not to impose her own needs on these wonderful people. Meir, Ayala, and David ordered coffee while Miriam settled on a glass of mint tea.

"Well, what would you suggest to a visitor?" Beth inquired.

"Definitely a falafel plate," said Meir.

Ayala's opinion was different, "Bubele, it might be too early for you to have a falafel plate, even though they are delicious. You might try their beautiful plate of fresh fruit and yogurt. Yogurt unlike anything you have ever had! I also believe there are a few almonds and other nuts on the plate as well."

Miriam and David remained silent on the subject, probably realizing that two different opinions were enough for Beth to contemplate. After a few seconds Beth said, "Meir, I think I will take you up on your suggestion this afternoon. It does sound wonderful but I will have to go with the fruit and yogurt plate."

After they had all ordered, Miriam began mapping out their day. First, they would go to their favorite stalls in the marketplace. She assured Beth that these would be the best places for Beth to buy a few groceries plus a few souvenirs, should she be interested. Beth definitely was interested in souvenirs and was grateful they had also thought of helping her buy some groceries. Miriam continued explaining that they would work their way back and stop for a light snack before heading home, mid-afternoon, for a requisite nap. Beth liked the sound of the entire schedule and sat back to enjoy her fruit plate. When it was time to leave, Meir insisted on picking up the bill and Beth graciously accepted.

The crowds were increasing and with them the noise was too. Beth loved listening to the haggling over prices and being able to walk up to each vendor and inspect his or her merchandise. Three stalls away from where they had breakfast, Beth found an espresso cup that she wanted to buy for Luke. She held it and smiled at the merchant. His head was wrapped in a white turban and he was wearing a long robe-like coat over a pair of trousers. His feet were sandaled and his smile genuine. "How much?"

"Twenty shekels," was his reply. Beth did some basic calculations and turned to Miriam.

"That is about five dollars, right?"

"Yes, that is about right, but you could bargain with him. He expects it, you know. Would you like me to?" Miriam offered.

"Oh no. I'm fine. That is very fair and I don't want to think that I couldn't pay a few extra cents for a present for my husband!"

Miriam and David smiled while Meir and Ayala continued looking at the merchant's other items. Beth reached into her pocket and handed over the shekels. The merchant held a brown bag in his hand, indicating that he could put the mug in it for Beth. She handed him the mug, waited the few seconds for him to wrap it, and moved towards the next stall. Meir and Ayala were a few steps behind.

The day continued with everyone eventually purchasing a few things. Beth bought a couple of ripe, mouth watering avocadoes. Miriam insisted she had the best recipe for them and would get the extra ingredients from Ayala's kitchen. She said there would be no reason for Beth to buy spices and other things of which she would only need a fraction.

At Meir's insistence, Beth also bought a cup or two of fresh grain cereal. She had never seen barrels filled with such items and bought them for the unique experience as much as for the product. At one of the stalls Beth actually bought a shopping bag. The entire Goldfarb clan protested, saying they had many extra ones but Beth wanted one of her very own and immediately put her purchases inside the canvas sack. She put the straps over her shoulder and knew that one final item would complete her purchases for the day.

Circling their way around, Beth spotted her prey: a long loaf of challah bread! Like a school girl, she ran to the vendor and pointed to the bread. All she could imagine was carrying her sack with the loaf of bread sticking out like a tried and true native. She fished for a few shekels and accepted her treasure. She turned to see David and Miriam laughing out loud at her escapade and Ayala and Meir smiling as if their only child was taking her first steps. Elizabeth, too, found herself laughing as they gathered together to confirm the last leg of their marketplace journey.

Being quite close to where they started their day, the final decision was to eat a light snack at a café about a dozen meters over from where they had eaten breakfast. Ayala wanted to make her own purchase from the outdoor shop that Beth had bought the cup for Luke. Ayala had been eyeing a tea service for four and had spent the day talking herself into and out of the purchase. For Ayala, a tea service represented time of love and laughter with friends and family. The set had to be perfect in many ways: how it felt, how it looked, and the feelings it evoked.

Having made up her mind to purchase the set, it was decided that they would all get a table and after they ordered, Miriam would run over and pick up the tea service for her mother.

Between the walking and shopping and bargaining, Beth had worked up quite an appetite. The sound of a plate of falafel sounded just right and she didn't need to ask anyone's opinion. David, too, seemed famished and ordered a corned beef sandwich and a cup of mushroom barley soup. Miriam limited her order to soup while Meir and Ayala ordered the same falafel plate as Beth. Once their order was in,

Miriam said, "Okay emma, I'll go and pick up the tea service. I'll be back in fifteen minutes."

"Sheyne meydele, I can't decide if I want the blue and white service or the green and white set. Let me go. I enjoy the walking and feel that I still have enough energy to walk one hundred meters!" Ayala was right; Beth had a difficult time keeping up with her at times. She did have a tremendous amount of stamina.

"How about if we go together?" Miriam asked.

"Tsk. Tsk. No, no. You keep our beautiful guest company. I don't want abba and David to bore her with talk of our economy or of our trials. You stay here and make our plans for tomorrow."

Like David, Miriam was incredibly respectful of her mother's wishes and simply said, "Okay, emma. That sounds like a good idea. We'll run our plans by you when you get back."

With that, Ayala left to buy her tea service, blue or green, and Miriam began discussing options for tomorrow's agenda. Miriam asked Beth what her hopes and expectations were for her trip and Beth shared what she wanted to accomplish within the next two weeks. She also worried, out loud, that she would become a burden to the Goldfarbs, or overstay her welcome. Miriam, David, and Meir simultaneously dismissed that notion and Beth knew they were sincere. *How had she been so blessed as to have found this wonderful family?*

With only a few blocks to home, Beth had ordered a glass of lemonade, as did the others. The drinks were delivered and the meal would soon be as well. Meir lifted his glass and held it towards Beth, Miriam, and David. With a twinkle in his eye he toasted, "Le Chaim. To Life."

David raised his glass, as did Miriam and Elizabeth. In unison they agreed, "Le Chaim. To Life."

Chapter Twelve

*Praise the Lord, who is so good;
God's love endures forever;
Praise the God of gods; God's love
endures forever;
Praise the Lord of lords; God's love
endures forever.
Psalm 136:1-3*

Nothing Beth had ever heard, or read, or thought, or imagined, or saw, or knew had prepared her for the next moment of her life. As they had raised their glasses to Meir's words of '*Le Chaim,*' an explosion simultaneously rocked the marketplace.

Everything was happening so quickly that Beth couldn't separate the sights and sounds, the screaming and yelling and crying. She couldn't breathe; her nostrils seemed to be on fire. Her eyes were burning from whatever was in the air. The back of her head prickled all over and when she touched it, her hand came away bloody. It began to throb but as soon as she noticed the pain, her attention was diverted to her friends at the table and then to everyone around her.

The impact of the bomb seemed to immediately set off sirens in the air and on the ground. Everywhere she looked, Beth saw terror. She was sure her heart was going to explode, making as horrific a mess as did the blast that just shook the marketplace. People were rushing through the streets, not knowing if they should run to help others or seek their own safety.

In the midst of the pandemonium, Beth looked at her dear friends around the table; Miriam, David, and Meir. She didn't know what she was looking for, maybe some sort of reassurance that this moment would quickly pass. That this wasn't near as terrible as it seemed to a visitor. However, searching their faces all Beth saw was complete and total pain. No words could ever describe their eyes. In an instant, they had changed from being full of life to being lifeless. Beth wanted to scream to them, *But we are alive! Let's leave this awful nightmare. Let's talk about our plans for tomorrow. If we ignore this it will go away. It has to!*

More than anything she had ever wanted in her whole entire life; Beth wanted to escape the horror of this moment. And then, time stopped. When it began again, it was slower, more methodical; there was no noise, no screaming, no sirens. Beth seemed to have joined Miriam and David and Meir in a different realm of existence. Her heart joined theirs. Their pain became her pain as she achingly realized that Ayala had been in the location of the blast. The terrible, horrible explosion happened very close to the stall where Beth had bought Luke's coffee cup, where Ayala had spotted the tea service and had gone to make a purchase.

Beth felt sick and thought she might become ill. She didn't know what to do as her body seemed to have a mind of its own. It wanted to collapse, to cry, to scream. Beth, however, wanted to say words of assurance to her sweet and kind friends. Beth prayed that her mouth would move and that somewhere from the depths of her soul would issue soothing words. But none came. Beth sat at the table waiting for the next explosion that would take her life. She was waiting for, she didn't know what she was waiting for, she was just waiting.

Slowly, then, succinctly, the mother in Beth took over. She pushed back her chair and moved to where Miriam also sat motionless. Beth crouched down in front of Miriam and held Miriam's hand. Beth's heart was filled with Ayala's love of Miriam as she realized that somehow, somewhere deep inside, Ayala knew, as she always did, with her intuitive sense, that she could not let Miriam purchase the tea set. Beth thought of her own daughter, Sophia, and knew that she would, without even thinking on it, put herself in harm's way to save her daughter, her sons, her children. As time stood still, Beth understood the great capacity to love that dwelt within a heart. The kind of love that Christ, Himself, must have felt to have offered His life for all.

Beth could see the entire scene replay in her mind's eye. Miriam offering to go make the purchase and Ayala saying something about being undecided on the color and having to go herself. And as Beth held Miriam's hand, Beth knew that it was one thing to console a daughter who has just lost a mother but it would have been something much worse to have had to console a mother about losing a daughter. And, in that instant, Beth understood how even in an awful tragedy, there could be gratitude.

Within minutes the ambulances and the police had filled the area. In a calm but firm way they were walking around, together, speaking with witnesses, sending people home, and investigating some of the minor injuries, like those at Beth's table. Holding Miriam's hand, Beth could see that the left side of Miriam's face had a few small abrasions where tiny drops of blood had dried in the ten excruciating minutes since the blast. They seemed to have been sitting at the very perimeter of the terrible explosion;

a safe enough distance to have kept their injuries to a minimum.

As Beth looked around, the same could be said of David, except his few cuts were on the other side of his face; his right side. And Meir had no apparent abrasions. This was because of the way they had been seated at their table. Beth's back was to the blast and with Miriam sitting to Beth's right, the left side of Miriam's face had sustained a minor cut or two from the debris that had flown through the air. Then, with David sitting across from Miriam, and at Beth's left, the right side of his face had sustained a few cuts as well. Because Meir was sitting directly across from Beth, but apparently blocked a good deal by Beth, he didn't seem to have any injuries in the physical sense. But looking at the pain in his eyes, Beth knew he would have traded places with Ayala in a heartbeat.

The police and paramedics walked up to their table and began questioning them in Hebrew. Beth gathered that David identified Beth as an American, or as a guest, as all eyes turned towards her. Their exchange lasted but a few minutes and ended with the police obviously giving condolences to the Goldfarbs. The sincerity of the moment brought the reality to light and all three Goldfarbs began crying. It wasn't a heart wrenching cry that Beth had so often seen on the television news. It was quiet, with no sobbing noises or motions. There were no hands waving in the air and no falling to the ground. And Beth saw that in the silence of their tears was the greatest grief of all.

Everyone remained mute, lost in his or her own sadness, as the paramedics tended to each of their cuts and scrapes. The paramedics suggested that they all ride to the hospital, just to be safe, but they declined; each knowing that their wounds were not of a physical nature. Then, when the paramedics walked away, Beth heard what sounded like a ripping noise. She turned and looked at David who had torn the collar of his shirt. Then Beth heard more ripping sounds as she watched Miriam and Meir do the same thing.

As the four of them turned and began walking home, Beth, too, tore her shirt. Mourning had begun.

Chapter Thirteen

*The way of the wicked is like darkness;
they know not on what they stumble.
But the path of the just is like shining
light, that grows in brilliance till perfect
day. Proverbs 4:18-19*

Luke woke up Sunday morning and lay in bed for a few minutes thinking of his Saturday afternoon with Joseph and Sammy. Sophia, it turned out, had to work and then was going to stay at the library to tackle a term paper. She left a note on the kitchen counter for Luke to read. Luke had gotten home from work by early afternoon and the boys were each playing on a computer. They had eaten cereal for breakfast and the house seemed to be in good shape. "Hey guys! How are you doing?" Luke had called out upon entering their home.

"Hey, dad," Sammy had responded from his upstairs bedroom. "I'm on my computer. How are you?"

Luke was thankful that Sammy hadn't quite entered his rebellious teenage years yet and still found it agreeable to talk to Luke and Beth. As expected, Joseph, more than ready to pick up the teen angst slack left by college-bound Michael, remained silent. "Joseph. Are you home?"

"Yeah," was Joseph's monosyllabic response.

"Anyone interested in going out to eat and then to a movie?" Luke waited for any indication that either boy could be pulled from his computer.

"Where?" Joseph asked.

A bit taken aback that Joseph was interested, Luke quickly responded, "Wherever you want. I'm game for anything. I haven't had lunch yet."

"What about Chinese?" Sammy inquired.

Luke, not really in the mood for Chinese food, wasn't about to let that deter the afternoon said, "Sounds good to me if it sounds good to you guys. What do you think, Joseph? Chinese?"

"Sure."

"Well, why don't you guys finish up your games and let's get going. I'm going to go get the mail, wash up, and put some jeans on. Do you guys think you can be ready in about twenty minutes?"

Sammy was the first to answer, "I just have to finish this battle. My guy's almost to the top. I'll be done in about five minutes."

Luke waited a few seconds for Joseph to chime in. Not hearing anything, Luke called up the stairs, "Joseph, what about you?"

"Five minutes," was the best Joseph could do in the way of an answer and Luke would take it.

"Sounds like a plan!"

Luke walked out to the mailbox and gathered the mail. A few pieces of junk mail went directly into the trash and then he carried the electric bill to his home office. Walking into the bedroom, Luke surveyed the mess that had already accumulated. He decided to throw in a load of wash before he and the boys headed out to eat. He also pulled the comforter up, onto the bed. He had never walked into their bedroom at the end of a workday and seen the bed unmade. It was an odd sight.

Walking over to the phone, Luke dialed the voice mail and found out that there was one message waiting to be heard. He knew the call had probably come in while he was at work and everyone else was asleep. Looking around his bedroom and admiring how Beth had decorated it, he dialed in to pick up the message.

The phone was on his side of the bed. Somehow, when chores and areas of responsibilities had been meted out in the early years of their marriage, the phone had become Luke's domain. He sat in the burgundy leather chair Beth had bought for him on their fifteenth wedding anniversary. While it wasn't as large as some leather chairs Luke had seen, it was the perfect size for their bedroom. Next to it sat a small end table that complimented their dark oak bedroom set. The corner was Luke's favorite spot for catching up on a few business-related articles at the end of the day.

Sitting in the chair, holding the phone to his ear, Luke looked at Beth's side of the bed. It also held a chair and a table, both complementing the bedroom furniture as well as Luke's chair. However, Beth's chair was not leather. Hers was the same burgundy color but made of a cotton fabric. Her table was empty, except for her lamp. She had taken the book from it and had also apparently packed the small family picture that had been taken at Michael's high school graduation. It was a beautiful picture with everyone smiling, almost on the verge of laughing. Something that had become quite rare of late.

"Hi honey. How are you? I'm fine and just wanted to check in. Today is Saturday and I am going to spend it with the Goldfarbs. We are going to attend service and then visit with some of their friends. The weather has been perfect and I have been blessed to have met such a wonderful family. I hope the boys are well and Sophia isn't taking on too much. Pay attention to her Luke. She's so busy sometimes she forgets to eat! I'll check in again in a day or two. Love to everyone!"

Luke finished listening to Liz's call, pressed the number to save the message, and changed into his jeans. Like Liz, Luke's waist had gained a few inches over the years, but he was still a fairly thin man. *Where had the time gone?* He wondered as he looked into the mirror. His hair was more gray than black and his heels often sore from heel spurs. All in all, though, life was very good. At least that was Luke's perspective. Lately, however, he had become painfully aware that Liz's perspective was quite different.

Walking through the kitchen towards the garage, Luke was surprised to see the boys. Rarely, if ever anymore, did they listen without multiple proddings. Luke took this as a good sign as they got into the SUV and headed towards the restaurant.

Luke pulled himself out of bed as he continued reflecting on yesterday's events. Dinner had been a success and the movie had been one they all enjoyed. It was some action packed story about an undercover cop who saves a family from tragedy. It had just enough violence to keep the boys interested but not so much as to upset Luke. And there was no sex in the movie, which was becoming a rarer occurrence with each passing year. These were the things, more than his gray hair and painful heels, which made Luke feel his age. Like Beth, Luke often wondered what kind of world his children were inheriting.

Making a pot of coffee, Luke looked at the clock and decided it would be good to take the kids to church. While the phone responsibilities had become his, church had somehow fallen into Liz's world of responsibilities. And Luke had not been too cooperative over the years. Now, for some reason,

Luke was feeling a real need to attend services today. He vaguely remembered that there was an eleven o'clock mass and decided that would be perfect. It would give the kids a couple more hours of sleep and still leave them all the afternoon for their own interests and obligations. Chances were that both boys had homework they had put off and Luke knew he needed to walk around and do a bit of cleaning. Sophia would be caught up on homework but would surely have other obligations to uphold. *Yep,* he thought, *church at eleven sounded great.*

Chapter Fourteen

I say to the Lord; You are my God;
listen, Lord, to the words of my prayers.
Psalm 140:7

Elizabeth woke up earlier than usual on Monday morning. Opening her eyes she was overcome with a mixture of emotions too great to bear. Her first thoughts were along the lines of relief that she had left a message for Luke Saturday morning and that she could get by another day or two without calling home. This would give her time to collect herself and arrive at a way to share what had happened without sending complete and total panic through Luke.

On the heels of relief were thoughts of sadness mingled with curiosity. *What should she do now? Should she ask the neighbors what might be expected of her? Should she consider herself part of the Goldfarb circle of friends and participate in the mourning process? Or should she extricate herself, quietly and without notice?* These questions hung in the air, above the bed, like the humidity of an August summer afternoon. Except now there were no lake breezes to remove the burdensome weight in the air, there was nothing Beth could do but suffer under the heaviness of it all.

Lying in bed, Beth decided that inaction might be her undoing and she forced herself to get up. The fog seemed to move with her from room to room. There was no escaping its powerful hold on her thoughts, her emotions. Walking into the bathroom, Beth stared at the clothes piled on the floor. She saw the droplets of blood, dried and darker than yesterday, staring back at her. She was immobilized by them. They ridiculed her inability to pull herself together, reveling in their power over her. Beth couldn't figure out why she had not just thrown them away and made her first conscious decision in fifteen hours.

Leaving the bathroom, Beth walked to the kitchen closet where she had seen a few garbage bags. Taking one in her hand, she walked back to the bathroom and began opening the bag. Picking up the clothes, Beth shoved them into the sack and tied it up, just like she had done hundreds, even thousands of times with the kitchen trash at home.

Beth thought about how the household chores had seemed to have been divided up over the years. Tying up the garbage bags from the kitchen and bathrooms had become Beth's job while taking the cans to the curb was Luke's. Once the garbage men picked up the trash, every Monday morning, Beth then dragged the empty cans back into the garage. How mundane it all seemed as she carried the tied sack to the front door. She knew she would never look at trash the same. What was wrong with her that she was thinking of her household chores when Meir and his children were making funeral arrangments for their mother? How completely befuddled had she become?

People often threw around the phrase, *life goes on*, but did they realize how it was both incredibly sad and hauntingly true at the same time? Yes, life was going on all the while the Israeli police were investigating the bombing and families were burying their dead. After that, what would there be? Families attempting to deal with their losses while others had long forgotten or moved on to the next day's headlines. Beth didn't know what was more tragic; that life did, indeed, go on, or the loss of life itself. Both seemed incredibly sad to her as she contemplated her own mortality.

Beth opened the door to the apartment to walk the trash to the building's receptacle on the main floor. She stopped at the door, put the bag down, and walked back into the bedroom. She remembered a newspaper stand outside the building and wanted to purchase a paper. She grabbed a handful of coins and decided she would try combinations until the machine opened. She also pulled on the overcoat that went with her loungewear. She knew she could get by with the outfit as it was a hybrid between a jogging suit and pajamas. Her feet were shod in slip-on canvas mules, also a cross between a shoe and a slipper. She picked up the keys off the hook by the kitchen and opened her door.

To her surprise and dismay, Beth almost ran into a neighbor who had a hand raised to knock on her door. She recognized the face but couldn't come up with a name. Staring at one another for what seemed an eternity, the woman finally spoke, "I am Ayala's neighbor, Mitzi, we've been introduced but I am sure you have met many of the Goldfarbs' friends over the past couple of days. I live down the hall." Mitzi was pointing in the direction opposite the elevator.

Beth obligingly looked down the hall and then turned her gaze to Mitzi. "Hello," was all Beth could come up with and had no facial expressions with which to accompany the salutation.

"I wanted you to know that Ayala has done nothing but talk about you since she met you." Tears welled up in Mitzi's eyes and Beth struggled to control her own emotions.

"Thank you for sharing that," Beth offered.

"The reason I tell you this is because the next seven days the Goldfarbs will be sitting Shivah. This will be their mourning period for Ayala. I know it would be very special to them if you could visit them during this time. They all seem to have fallen in love with you. I wanted to share this with you because I thought you might not know how they feel about you and how good it would be for you to see them."

The fog seemed to lift from Beth's brain and she hugged Mitzi. Tears now streamed uncontrollably down Beth's face as she said, "Thank you for letting me know. I will be there for them. They have been so warm and caring to me I feel like they are my family."

Mitzi gave Beth a short explanation of what the next week would hold. She told Beth what to expect when she entered the Goldfarb home; mirrors would be covered, David and Meir would be unshaven, all would go without the luxury of showers as they honor the life of their mother. Mitzi told Beth that everyone would be sitting on low stools, or even the floor, and that there was a traditional greeting that is said to a mourner.

"Please teach me this greeting," Beth all but pleaded with Mitzi.

"I'll tell you what," Mitzi said. "You finish what you were doing and come over to my apartment for a cup of coffee. I will teach you the greeting."

"That would be so kind of you. I will be there in half an hour."

They parted ways and Beth watched which apartment Mitzi walked into because when she had originally pointed down the hall, she could have been indicating one of two apartments that were at the end. Once Beth saw the correct apartment, she took her clothes to the garbage bin and bought herself the current edition of The Jerusalem Post's Christian edition. Glancing at the headlines, she folded the paper in half, with the screaming words and horrific pictures on the inside. Opening her door, she placed the paper on the kitchen counter and walked to the bathroom. Deciding that she would stay in the outfit she was wearing, she brushed her teeth, ran a comb through her hair, splashed water on her face, and headed to Mitzi's apartment.

Knocking on Mitzi's door Beth found herself entertaining odd thoughts. *How fortunate am I that everyone speaks such fluent English?*

Mitzi opened the door and ushered Beth into the kitchen. She was talking in hushed tones and immediately explained, "My husband has not been feeling well and is still in bed." Beth nodded her head in understanding. It was a small apartment and a little noise would carry a long way.

Mitzi had prepared a fresh pot of coffee and there were two cups on the table. There was also a tray that held bagels, smoked salmon, some garnishes, and a few slices of cheese. "Please, let us eat. I know Ayala would never settle for you going hungry!"

As they each made themselves a small plate of food, Mitzi continued sharing some of the customs and practices of Shivah. Beth knew that Mitzi would welcome any questions from Beth, but Beth didn't seem to have enough energy to get the words from her brain to her mouth. The fog was deep in her brain cells. She was hoping that Mitzi wouldn't question what Ayala had seen in her.

"There will often be at least ten men gathered in the Goldfarb home throughout the next week. Ten men constitute a 'minyan' and are important because we believe that this is how God calls us together to pray. This is especially important so that the Kaddish can be said."

Beth remembered Kaddish from Saturday's synagogue service and heard David's explanation rattling around in her head.

"Everyone will bring food to the Goldfarb's and you will see that after tomorrow's funeral service the main food will be bread and hard-boiled eggs. There will also be chickpeas and bagels. These foods, being circular in nature, remind us of the never ending cycle of life and death. It is something we feel blessed by and we remember how great our Creator is."

Beth was struck by another of her odd thoughts and blurted it out before her brain had a chance to grab it, "Will David still become a rabbi?" For some reason Beth knew this was very important to Ayala and, having seen the pride and joy in Ayala's face when she talked of David's decision, knew that Ayala would want David's plans to continue.

"I am sure, more than ever before, David will become a rabbi and will honor his mother's life and death in all that he does."

Beth knew that Mitzi was right and was thankful that Mitzi hadn't given her a puzzled look at the peculiar question. "Would you please teach me the greeting now?"

Mitzi smiled and knew why Ayala had taken such a liking to this young woman. She was clearly affected by the terrible tragedy and wanted, so very much, to share in the family's grief, maybe hoping to alleviate it even one miniscule bit. "I will say it a few times; first as it is said, then I will say it slowly. Then I will say it word by word and have you repeat it after me? Would that be good?"

The teacher in Beth liked the format of the lesson and agreed.

Mitzi began, "Ha-Makom yinakhem otkha b'tokh sh'ahr avalei Tzion v'Yerushalayim. This means, 'May the Almighty comfort you among the mourners of Zion and Jerusalem.'"

Elizabeth's lesson continued for more than twenty minutes while she mastered the phrase. This was very important to her and she prayed that it would somehow show the Goldfarbs that her heart ached for them and for the loss of Ayala.

Chapter Fifteen

*A thousand years in your eyes are merely
a yesterday. But humans you return to
dust, saying, "Return, you mortals!"*
Psalm 90:3-4

Mitzi had done a masterful job in explaining Shivah to Beth. For two days Beth was very much part of the Goldfarb clan. She was not at all surprised at the number of friends they had, even though their family was small. Beth also found out that a typical Jewish funeral was held within twenty-four hours of death but that Ayala's had been delayed an extra day to allow family from the states to arrive.

At the end of the second day Beth knew she had to make a call to Luke. If too much time passed, he would be beside himself and that wouldn't do her kids any good. Beth knew that Luke would be paying special attention to news about the Middle East and that any report of the recent bombing would have him frantic.

Although she wasn't anxious to share the awful news, she made the call. She also knew that she couldn't get by with leaving another message. That was the coward's way out and Luke deserved better.

The phone rang three times. One more time and voicemail would pick up.

"Hello?" Luke answered.

"Hi! How are you?" Beth sincerely wanted to know.

"We are doing great. Doing my best to keep the house up for you. Enjoying time with the boys. Catching a glimpse of Sophia as she runs from here to there. Hey, did you know that conferences were this week?" Luke had obviously not heard news of the explosion.

Beth had actually forgotten about conferences and said so.

"No biggie. I can make it. Meghan is enjoying my shortened schedule because it is giving her more time off!"

"Well hopefully that shortened schedule will still be working for you when I get back so that I can enjoy it too." Beth cringed at the words and yet felt they were spoken in all honesty. She did hope that Luke would shorten his hours so that they could get to know each other again.

The sarcasm wasn't lost on Luke who remained silent for a few seconds before saying, "So, what kind of sights have you been enjoying?"

This was it; Beth's opening to somehow share what had been happening during her stay in Israel. "Well," she began. "I'm not sure where to begin so I'll just go ahead and say this. You know the Goldfarbs, the family who has been so gracious to me? Well, on Sunday, at the end of our day at the marketplace, there was an explosion and Ayala was killed."

Luke's previous silence had been a warm up act for what now followed. Beth wasn't sure if she should continue talking or wait for him to digest what she had just said. She opted to wait. She thought of the countless times she had seen people interviewed on television and how a reporter would masterfully let an interviewee speak endlessly, hanging him or herself in the interim. Beth didn't want the same thing happening to her and restrained herself from offering further information until asked.

After a full minute, Luke asked in rapid succession, "Are you okay? Are you hurt? Who set off the explosion?"

All legitimate questions, Beth thought, and since she had never opened the paper to get more information about the event was able to honestly say, "I'm fine. I'm not physically hurt. And, I don't know who was behind this."

Silence preceded Luke's next question which took Elizabeth by surprise. "How are her husband and children? That must be a horrible thing to go through."

Every once in a while Luke did this to Beth. She expected to have to fight to remain in Israel and here her husband was inquiring as to the well-being of the surviving Goldfarbs. She was touched. "Considering the circumstances, they are as well as can be expected."

"I assume you want to finish your stay? Or do you want to come home early? Beth, your obligation is to your family." Beth could tell from the tremor in Luke's voice that he was pacing the floor and choosing his words very carefully. Luke was a very protective man, both to her and to the children. Sophia's dates dreaded it when Luke was home. He was never overtly rude to them but he never, ever went out of his way to make them feel welcome.

In some ways it felt suffocating but in other ways it was comforting. Mostly it depended on Beth's mood as Luke remained the same throughout their married life. He was a rock. He loved and cared for his family unlike anyone Beth had ever known.

"No, I don't want to come home early. I want to stay. I want to offer my help in any way. These are wonderful people Luke and if it is at all possible, I feel like I have known them forever."

"Beth, I don't agree with that decision. It is one thing to hear of tragic events but quite another to have been involved, first hand. I believe you need to come home."

Beth knew Luke needed to see that she was safe and would remain safe while in Israel. She wanted to reassure him but didn't know how. Life felt more and more like happenstance, chance, luck of the draw, and she knew there were no words to allay Luke's fears.

"Luke, please, I do not want to come home yet. I want to finish my trip, as planned. So, what have you guys been doing?"

Luke remained silent, obviously weighing the pros and cons of boarding a plane and forcefully bringing his wife back home. Not happy with Beth's decision but knowing that it was firm, he proceeded to tell Elizabeth that he had been somehow inspired to take the children to church on Sunday. Beth felt that there was no coincidence in the timing. The Lord knew she would need to be covered in prayers and Luke had responded to the call. They were more connected than she had realized.

They finished their conversation with Beth asking about Michael and to speak to Sophia, Joseph, and Sammy. She spent a few minutes telling them how much she loved them and then hung up. Sammy told her that Luke had taken over her "tucking in" responsiblities but that he wasn't near as good as she was. Sammy had always liked his back rubbed a certain way and that had been Elizabeth's job from the start but she had to admire Luke for giving it the old college try.

When Beth hung up the phone, it was late in the day. She languidly moved around the apartment. There had been a silent stand-off between her and the paper on the counter. After the first glance at the headlines, she had folded the paper in half, headlines inside, and had yet to open it. Still not ready, she walked past it and into the kitchen for a glass of water.

She couldn't remember if she had eaten any dinner and rummaged through the cupboards. Nothing there. Mitzi had given her a small bag of groceries and Beth had loaded them into the refrigerator without really paying attention. Opening the refrigerator door Beth saw, with tremendous gratitude, a few containers of hummus, tabouli, and cheese. There was a box of matzoh in the cupboard and she made herself a nice, light meal. She sat at the table and looked out at the city. *How could such a holy and anointed place hold such sadness and tragedy?* She couldn't get over the inconsistency.

Getting up, Beth walked into the kitchen and washed her lone plate and fork. There was still food in the containers in the fridge and she knew Mitzi wouldn't mind if it were a day or two until they were returned. One common denominator Beth had found among everyone she had met was that, without an exception, they were all truly giving people. Nothing was said without sincerity. If someone offered to do something for you, he or she meant it.

There was great peace in that knowledge and Beth made a pact with herself to work on that trait. She had always been the kind of person to offer this or that and then felt overwhelmed if taken up on her offers. From now on she would offer her time or effort and consider it a "mitzvah" if she was then called upon to deliver. She needed more mitzvahs and less stress. Mitzi and Ayala and Miriam and all the Goldfarb friends and neighbors had shown her how to embrace the opportunities God gave for each and every one of us to do good deeds for one another.

Chapter Sixteen

*Return, my soul, to your rest; the Lord
has been good to you. Psalm 116:7*

The third day of Shivah was underway as was
Beth's morning routine. Before she knew it, she was
at the Goldfarb door, ready to offer her help, sit
silently as needed, or just plain show that their
mother had been a magnificent woman.

Beth was startled when Miriam answered the
door and, instead of opening it wide enough for Beth
to enter, had closed the door behind her as she stood
in the hall. "Beth, both my father and brother and I
have talked about this and want you to know that
this is your vacation. You have been more than
generous with your time during our Shivah but you
must go and enjoy our country."

Miriam held her hand up to Beth as Beth
started to protest. "We could not live with the fact
that this is the bulk of your trip to our beloved
country. We have called some friends and they have
shown a great desire in taking you to some of the
spots you had talked about. We know you want to
see the Western Wall and the Temple Mount and so
many other things. One of our best friends is a
Christian Jew and could think of nothing better than
spending the next few days with you, sharing these
experiences. We hope this is okay as we have made
arrangments for them to pick you up this afternoon."

Beth didn't know if she should be hurt or
pleased. She opted for humbly pleased and thanked
Miriam. She assured Miriam that nothing had been
more important to her than spending time sitting

Shivah with them. Elizabeth wanted Miriam to share with David and Meir that never, not once, did she think of doing anything other than spending time with them. It seemed clear, based on Miriam's response, that they all knew this and Beth was relieved. She couldn't live with the idea that any of them would believe she could think of herself during their time of grief.

Miriam told her that Rachel and Sipporah would be by around noon to pick her up. Rachel had apparently been Miriam's professor at the university and Sipporah was one of Miriam's classmates. That meant that Rachel would be close to Beth's age and that Sipporah would be somewhere close to Miriam's age, which was still a mystery to Beth.

Miriam hugged Beth and turned to go inside. "By the way," she began. "You will love the way Rachel will bring your messiah to life for you!" and then Miriam closed the door.

Beth was more than a little intrigued by Miriam's parting comment. Opening the door to her own apartment, she looked at the clock. She had a full two hours before her newly appointed tour guides would arrive. Emboldened by the morning, Beth walked over to the paper and lifted it from its prone position.

Slowly opening it, as if it were a bomb, Beth read the headlines, "Eleven People Killed In Bomb Blast at Market." Walking and reading at the same time, Beth found out that the blast had killed Israelis and Arabs alike. The article postulated who or what group might have been behind the attack. But that's all it was, guesses. No one had claimed responsibility and authorities were working on the few meager tips they had received. Beth thought of the kind eyes of the Arab who had owned the shop and said a prayer for his family. So many people had been affected by this that she didn't know how to wrap her mind around it all. *How would it all end?* She kept asking herself. *Who held the answer?*

Beth walked over to the living room recliner and settled in to finish her reading. As she completed the article on the blast that had killed Ayala, she read each of the victim's names out loud and said a prayer for their peaceful eternal rest. She also said a prayer for each of their families. She wondered if they were all in heaven. *Was heaven even a real place? If it was, were these people who had been enemies on earth now friends?* Her mind was quickly filling up with errant thoughts when she heard a tapping on the door. Pushing the chair to an upright position, she walked across the room to answer the knock.

Opening the door, she was greeted by Mitzi's husband, whose name currently escaped her. "Hello," she said, hoping he wouldn't mind that she didn't use his name.

Smiling as he handed over a grocery bag, he said, "Mitzi wanted to make sure you were eating."

Beth graciously accepted the bag and murmured her gratitude. It seemed as though Mitzi, in honoring Ayala's memory, was determined to ensure Beth's nutritional needs were met.

Opening the bag, she noticed a container of fresh fruit compote and a jar of matzoh ball soup. Mouth watering, Beth took a bowl from the cupboard and filled it with the fruit which she ate while the soup heated up on the stove. All the while Beth was pondering the sadness in her heart. There was a piece of her heart that ached due to the death of Ayala and the sadness with which her family would have to cope. But there was another piece of her heart that felt an ache for an entirely different reason.

Beth was probing and prodding the melancholy feeling she had regarding the aftershock of Ayala's passing, trying to name it or identify it in some way. *Shouldn't Beth have wanted to run home to Luke after this experience? Why was Beth not running for the comfort of home during this tragedy?* Somewhere in the midst of the past three days Beth put her own needs aside and was more interested in how she could help meet the needs of the Goldfarbs. Now she felt tied to them in ways untold. *You don't share what we just did and walk away from it,* Beth told herself.

The soup was near boiling before Beth noticed it on the stove. Startled back to reality, she turned the stove off and poured the piping hot soup into a bowl. Now she would have to wait for it to cool down. She decided to step out onto the balcony and listen to the city speak to her.

She had grown to love the sounds she heard from the balcony, they were so different from anything she had ever experienced at home, in her backyard. This is why people fell in love with cities like New York and Chicago. There was a life coming from those cities that could not be tamed. Its pulse becoming the pulse of its inhabitants, ebbing and flowing, day and night, a crescendo at times while on other occasions a mere lull. Jerusalem was magnificent.

Knowing she had given her soup enough time to cool down, Beth went back inside. She silently thanked Mitzi while she ate the best matzoh ball soup ever. Her local deli had nothing on the kitchens in Jerusalem! She had just finished washing out her two bowls and spoons when there was a knock on the door. Drying her hands, Beth answered the door.

"Shalom. You must be Beth. I am Rachel and this is Sipporah. We are friends of Miriam's and your guides for the next few days."

She looked at the two women standing at the door and smiled. Rachel was a bit older than Beth had expected, maybe by a few years. Her beautiful dark black hair was peppered with gray around the temples and strands making their way through the sides. The cut was short, just making it to her ears where she had it tucked behind. Her blue eyes sparkled with kindness and a bit of mischief as she was obviously looking forward to sharing her city with Beth.

Sipporah looked to be about ten years younger than Beth and had thick blonde hair with brown eyes. Her hair was long and hung in front of her shoulders and behind. Like Rachel, she was Beth's height. In fact, all three of them couldn't have been more than an inch different than the others. Sipporah looked like an athlete with muscular arms and calves showing in her Capri pants and short sleeve t-shirt. She had a sweater tied around her neck and her shoes were plain white sneakers. They both looked completely ready for a day of sight seeing.

Grinning from ear to ear, Beth said, "Yes, I'm Beth. I'm delighted to meet you both! Let me just get my sweater and purse and we'll be on our way."

Chapter Seventeen

*Pleasing words are a honeycomb, sweet to
the taste and healthful to the body.*
Proverbs 16:24

Elizabeth didn't know where to start a conversation and decided, once again, to take her cue from the news interviews. She remained silent as they walked down the stairs and out the front door. The day was slightly overcast, with rain suggested by the clouds. Beth was glad she brought a sweater although figured it would be worthless against a hearty downpour. She thought of the phrase, 'worth a plug nickel' and then spent time wondering what a plug nickel was and why it was worthless. Had it always been worthless, she asked herself. *Who knew?* She smiled to herself as she heard that faint rise in inflection, just as Ayala had always done. *Who knew, indeed?*

Even though it was a rhetorical question, sometimes Beth really did want to ask someone, anyone, *Who knew? Who knew the answers to some of life's big questions?* At forty eight she was starting to feel that she had more questions than answers. Somehow it felt that the cosmic order of things was completely unbalanced. *Weren't mothers supposed to have all the answers? Weren't mothers supposed to be fearless and indomitable?*

Rachel broke the silence, and Beth's mental ramblings, with a topic that affected all three women, Ayala. "Miriam has been almost inconsolable. We are very worried about her. Her mother was an angel and we will all miss her kind words and caring gestures. Since Miriam's incident, Ayala has been at her side day and night. If it wasn't for Ayala, Miriam never would have survived such a thing."

Sipporah could tell by Beth's face that Beth was in the dark about Miriam's incident. Sitting in the back seat of the small car they had gotten into, Sipporah sent Rachel a look in the rear view mirror that said, *Shh! You've said too much.* Sipporah quickly changed the subject. "Beth, Miriam tells us you have three teenage sons and a teenage daughter! What a job you have with them, no?"

Beth loved the way Sipporah used the word 'no' at the end of her sentence. "Yes, I have quite a job, but really, they are good children. Just like all kids, wanting to see that you mean what you say and you say what you mean." Beth wondered if her children felt about her the way that Miriam felt about Ayala. It was difficult to tell with teenagers, especially boys. Sophia, on the other hand, tended to make her feelings quite clear. Beth thought of her time with her children. One minute she was laughing and joking with them and the next minute she was their arch enemy. *Who knew?*

It was exhausting, truth be told, but Beth kept that to herself. In no small way they were part of the reason for her excursion. It seemed as if motherhood had very few perks and even fewer accolades. If Beth waited around until her kids were old enough to show their appreciation, well, she often said she wouldn't actually see that day, having had her children in her thirties and all. People loved to hear Beth's humor in regards to mothering but she needed to be replenished before she could go on. She felt like Mike had taken a lot out of her during his junior and senior high school years and now Sophia and Joseph often seemed to be vying to pick up where Michael had left off. Yes, she was a parched desert traveler and felt that the Holy Land was calling to her, to quench her thirst.

"Well, I am sure that your children are wonderful but know that you came to the Holy Land for a reason and we are here to help you see the sights most precious in your heart and to share some of our own favorites with you. When you go back home you will be filled with a new joy and a new spirit." Beth listened to Rachel and wondered if Rachel had mind reading capabilities.

"What did you have planned for today?" Beth inquired.

"Well, maybe we should ask you if you have anything that you feel you can't leave without seeing and we can go from there."

"Hmm...Let's see...okay...I really want to see the Wailing Wall, the Garden Tomb, The Church of the Holy Sepulcher, and Via Dolorosa. What do you think?"

"This is no problem! You have a made a nice list for yourself and we would be glad to help you see and enjoy those places. If you don't mind, we could also offer a few of our own suggestions. I am on a sabbatical from the university right now and Sipporah is putting the final touches on her term papers so we are both quite available over the next week. It would be a mitzvah to be your guide."

"I honestly don't know what to say. Although I have only been here but a few days, it is if I have lived here my whole life and have the best friends in the world!"

All three women smiled knowingly. There were times when God just opened the heavens and showered you with riches and this was one of those times.

Within a few minutes, Rachel was parking her small car. "This is as far as we can go by car. The rest we will cover by foot. Cars are not allowed. I believe the perfect place to begin is the walk of Christ, or what is called Via Dolorosa. It begins here, at St. Stephen's Gate in the Muslim Quarter. It winds through with a number of spots marked for the different stations and then ends in the Christian Quarter, at the Holy Sepulcher."

Beth was already beside herself with excitement. "Why is this called St. Stephen's Gate?"

She listened with rapt attention as both Sipporah and Rachel took turns explaining how Old City was constructed. Beth was told that there were seven gates from which a visitor could enter the area. Each one named according to its unique location or because of a particular characteristic. For instance, The Jaffa Gate faces West towards Tel Aviv and Joppa while The Damascus Gate, located in the northern wall, was where a traveler would enter if he or she had come from Galilee, the Golan Heights and Damascus.

The Zion Gate is located on Mt. Zion, near the Tomb of David and by the Upper Room where Christ celebrated the Last Supper. The Dung Gate, aptly received its name from its history as it faced south towards the Hinnom Valley, where refuse had been dumped in early days. They would be entering through the Sheep Gate, also known as St. Stephen's Gate or the Lion's Gate. It was located next to a sheep market.

Beth liked the symbolism of entering the Old City via The Sheep's Gate. Wasn't she, after all, one of His flock? It made so much sense that Beth felt giddy.

As they began their tour through the narrow streets of Old City, Rachel and Sipporah continued sharing their wealth of information with Beth. The tour began with the first station at The Monastery of the Flagellation, marking Jesus being condemned to death.

Rachel pointed to the sign indicating the path and Beth felt quite thankful to have such a knowledgeable guide. Rachel told Beth that there were a few opinions on the route but that they would follow the most common procession. Beth could see that the route itself was going to afford little, if any, time for prayer and mediation. The narrow streets were filled with people and merchandise, both of which fascinated Beth.

Sipporah made sure that Beth saw the two small chapels. The one on their right called The Chapel of Flagellation which is where Christ was beaten. The chapel on their left being called The Chapel of Judgment and is where Pilate's judgment was made again Jesus.

"Would you like to step inside the Chapel for a moment?"

Beth quickly agreed that she would and the three women stepped inside the small chapel. Taking a back pew, the women sat for a few minutes, each lost in her thoughts. Sipporah was the first to move, gesturing toward the door so as to avoid distracting the other occupants of the church. Rachel and Beth quietly followed Sipporah out of the church.

Once outside they turned south and passed one of the northwestern gates of the Temple Mount. Although Beth knew most of what Rachel and Sipporah were explaining, she listened nonetheless. Sipporah was speaking about the Temple Mount as the place where Abraham brought Isaac, in following

God's instructions, and would have sacrificed Isaac had not an angel stopped his hand. Rachel ruminated about the difficulties in following God's will and Beth lamented the often difficult task of discerning it before it could be followed. All three women wholeheartedly agreed.

"Don't forget that the Temple Mount is also of great significance to our Muslim brothers and sisters. This is where their great prophet Muhammad ascended to his father in heaven. It is where the Dome of the Rock is built, the third holiest place on earth to the people of Islamic faith."

Beth was impressed at Sipporah's compassionate way of speaking about Muslims, calling them 'brothers' and 'sisters' and wanted to know what the first and second most holiest places were for the Muslims.

"That would be Mecca and Medina," answered Sipporah.

Rachel explained that Sipporah's parents were that rare mix of Christian and Muslim. She didn't offer who was of what faith and Beth didn't feel it was right to ask. Sipporah also didn't offer details about her life in a Jewish nation with parents who were Christian and Muslim, but Beth could only imagine. "Well," Beth began without thinking. "We certainly have our bases covered!"

Laughing, Sipporah said, "We sure do!" With station two having been in close proximity to station one, they were now nearing station three; marked by a relief sculpture above the door of a little Polish chapel. Station three is where Jesus fell, under the weight of the cross, for the first time.

Very close to station three was station four. The Armenian Church of Our Lady of the Spasm marked the site. Beth, Rachel, and Sipporah went inside so that Rachel could point out in the mosaic floor, an outline that was said to be that of Mary's sandals. Looking at the imprints, Beth realized that it actually did not matter if they were or weren't what they were purported to be. For Beth, these small points of contention were introduced to change a person's focus, which was supposed to be on Christ.

The fifth station, almost part of a group that included stations three and four, was where Simon of Cyrene was forced by Roman soldiers to help Jesus carry this cross. Beth knew this to be from Matthew 27:32 and Mark 15:21, as well as Luke 23:26. These had become Beth's favorite, or maybe she would have said most relevant, scripture verses over the past couple of years as she did her best to understand her oldest son's belligerence and her own discontent. Everyday Beth tried to honor God by taking up her cross.

From the fifth station the women began an uphill walk through narrow streets towards the sixth station, where Veronica wiped Jesus' face. Pilgrims, like Beth, filled the street. Once in a while Beth would catch a glimpse of a child skipping or laughing. The simple beauty of such a sight clarified why Christ would have said that the kingdom belonged to such as these. She smiled at the memories of her own children, as youngsters, enjoying a day in the park or a bike ride through the neighborhood.

While they walked Rachel shared a bit of the history of the walled city with Beth. "The Walls of the Old City were built by an Ottoman ruler named Suleiman. He lived in the mid 1500's and built the wall, after he had conquered the Jewish people, because he believed he would be killed by lions if he did not. So, he enclosed the city.

Today there are four areas inside: the Muslim Quarter, the Jewish Quarter, the Christian Quarter, and the Armenian Quarter. The Arab market runs throughout and gives the city its vibrancy and appeal. You feel like you have walked back in time when you visit the Old City. "

Beth completely agreed as they worked their way up the steep hill to station six. She noticed that the uphill climb was a bit of a challenge and was glad that she had worn short sleeves with an optional sweater, which now hung loosely tied around her waist. She bent over to pick up a stone and turned it around in her hand before dropping it gently back to the ground. To be walking in Christ's last steps was almost incomprehensible to her.

"Earlier I mentioned the gates that you could use to enter the city but did not mention the gates which are not in use. Of particular importance, and a main attraction for tourists, is the Golden Gate. It is located in the east portion of the wall. It is where many Jews believe the Messiah will arrive. For Christians it is where Christ is expected to return and for Muslims it is where divine judgment will occur. So, you can see how important that gate is to billions of people worldwide!"

"Why couldn't we use that gate to enter?" Beth asked.

"That gate was sealed by Suleiman," Sipporah laughingly answered. "Suleiman thought he could prevent the Messiah from arriving by blocking His expected entrance!" Beth and Rachel also chuckled at such an idea.

As their laughter subsided, they found themselves at the sixth station. And none too early as far as Beth was concerned. While she wanted to know a bit more about the Golden Gate, she was ready for a rest. Station six also had a church, The Church of the Holy Face. Once again, all three women stepped inside for a moment of prayer.

As they sat down, Beth wondered if Sipporah was a practicing Christian or a Muslim. She knew, based on what Miriam had said that Rachel was a Christian Jew. For the first time ever, Beth showed great restraint in letting this all go. She decided that these things would reveal themselves, in God's time, over the next few days. Right now she just wanted to enjoy her few minutes at The Church of the Holy Face.

Leaving the church, they headed on a ways, towards the Franciscan church marking the seventh station; where Jesus fell a second time. They moved in unison, silence peacefully settling upon them as the weight of Jesus' last hours began to manifest in their minds and in their hearts. Even Miriam had once mentioned being affected by thoughts of Christ's suffering and tortuous death.

As Beth approached station eight, the words of Jesus rang through her ears as she recalled Luke 23:27-31, *A large crowd of people followed Jesus, including many women who mourned and lamented him. Jesus turned to them and said, "Daughters of Jerusalem, do not weep for me; weep instead for yourselves and for your children, for indeed, the days are coming when people will say, 'Blessed are the barren, the wombs that never bore and the breasts that never nursed.' At that time people will say to the mountains, 'Fall upon us!' and to the hills, 'Cover us!' for if these things are done when the wood is green what will happen when it is dry?"*

There weren't many Scripture verses that Beth had committed to heart, but the few that were reflected in the stations had become a very large part of her life of late. Beth stared across from station eight and saw a cross with the Greek inscription NIKA on the wall of a Greek Orthodox Monastery.

Silence was now the fourth member of their group and the women moved to station nine. It was at the Coptic Patriarchate next to the Church of the Holy Sepulchre. The site of Jesus' third fall was identified by a Roman pillar. Beth's heart started picking up its pace as her eyes took in the church.

The remaining five stations of the Via Dolorosa were inside this ancient church. Many people believe that Jesus was buried and raised from the dead on this very spot. It is, by most, to be considered the holiest site in Christianity. Beth traveled half way around the world to stand on this ground and the significance was palpable.

"The silence we have shared will feel like chaos compared to the beautiful silence you will feel once you step inside this church," Rachel offered in a hushed voice. "I know you have probably done your homework before taking this trip but I wonder if I might give you information about the church before we enter and then you will be free to walk around, pray, do as you wish or as God wishes you to while you are inside this sanctuary."

Rachel had been right; Beth did her homework, so to speak, but was unaware as to the specifics of the church. All she knew was that it was shared by a few different denominations. "Yes, please share with me some of the details of the church and then we will go inside." Sipporah took a few steps off the walk so that they could gather and speak without hindering pilgrims making their way to the church.

Rachel then began, "As you know, Golgotha, or Calvary, is where Jesus was crucified. Constantine, the first Roman Christian ruler, built this church over the area where Jesus' crucifixion, burial, and resurrection occurred. As you know from our walking, we are now on a hilltop and it is here that Roman Catholics celebrate the tenth station.

Interestingly, the church has been split into two parts. The left area belongs to the Greek Orthodox and the right to the Roman Catholics. But you will also see that in many ways it is like a large building that houses many small churches. The building seems to change with every turn you take because of these different hands lovingly taking care of it.

Actually, as a result of the many different Christian denominations that are under this one roof, the main key was given, in 1192, to a Muslim family, who became guardians of the door with the responsibility to open and close it every day. At one point another family, the Joudehs, was brought in and entered into the current arrangement; that a member of the Joudeh family brings the key to a member of the Nuseibeh family, who then opens the door!"

Thinking of the struggles between her own children, Beth couldn't help but chuckle at such an arrangement and yet was taken aback at the solemnity of the centuries old tradition. Rachel nodded as if to say, *Amazing, isn't it?* and continued on, "Immediately inside you will see magnificent lamps suspended over the Stone of Unction. The stone honors the preparation of Jesus' body for burial and the lamps hanging above it have been donated by various denominations. The stone itself is a polished limestone that dates from 1808 when the prior slab was destroyed.

This sacred site, who most agree is, in actuality, worthy of its claim, belongs to the four main sects; Armenians, Copts, Greeks, and Latins. It is about the length of an average size man and maybe two or so feet wide and is at the foot of Golgotha. You can so easily imagine our crucified Savior lying on the slab and that is why you will see visitors weeping for their Savior at this spot.

They are immersing themselves into that point in time and mourning His death, knowing that He loved them to such a degree as to offer His life for their sins. It tends to make visitors pause, whether in sorrow or in regret, for the sins of their lives.

Moving on, you will see that the tenth station is venerated at the top of the stairs, leading to Calvary, where Jesus was stripped of his garments. Each step you take will feel like a step you are taking with Christ and you will enter your own communion with Him during this time. I have walked this many times and have witnessed, over and over again, how pilgrims seem to transcend time and space, just as you do during the transubstantiation of Eucharist at your mass.

The eleventh station is at the silver altar where Jesus was nailed to the cross. My first pilgrimage here, I felt the heartache of the visitors who wept for the pain they felt they had inflicted upon Christ through their sins."

Beth felt as if she could bear no more and wondered if she would actually be able to walk these last stations. *What have I done to cause Him such pain?* She asked herself, knowing that her sins were both in what she had done in life but also in what she had failed to do. Rachel saw Beth's inner turmoil and offered words of comfort, "You will be okay Beth. Not every Christian can take this journey and you are very blessed to be able to do so. The Lord will be with you and reveal to you His love during these last few stations unlike anything you have experienced before. Remember that He died for you so that you may be resurrected with Him."

Beth smiled at Rachel's kind words and nodded for her to continue explaining the last few stations.

"The twelfth station is on the Greek Orthodox altar. It is where our Lord and Savior died upon the cross. There is a limestone rock underneath marking where Jesus' cross stood as well as the crosses of the two thieves who were crucified with Him. The great schism which was caused by the earthquake that took place at the time of Christ's death is also visible. As much as I turn to Scripture for knowledge of these sites, this particular one always makes me think of the beautiful C.S. Lewis tale, "The Lion, the Witch, and the Wardrobe" where the stone altar breaks apart after the lion is sacrificed. Mr. Lewis was a magnificent writer."

Beth agreed with Rachel as she recalled reading the entire C.S. Lewis series with her children when they were younger. She loved how Lewis had crafted such a novel, rife with Christianity.

Rachel finished explaining how the Roman Catholic side marked the thirteenth station, where Jesus was taken down from the cross and that it was commemorated at the altar of Our Lady of Sorrows. She shared that below Calvary was the Chapel of St. Adam which memorialized the parallel between Adam, the first man, through whom the human race first sinned, and Jesus Christ, the new Adam, through whom we have our salvation. She finished by suggesting that it was time to step inside and allow their spirits be guided by God.

Beth and Sipporah agreed and the three approached the door. Opening it, Beth half expected to be lifted off her feet and swept up into the heavens. She was more than ready for this moment and stepped inside.

Chapter Eighteen

Unless the Lord builds the house, they labor in vain who build. Psalm 127:1

Luke was having a much more difficult time with Liz's absence than he would have thought. The boys seemed a bit more subdued in their behavior towards one another and the house had a cavernous feel to it where her energy was missing. Luke sat at his desk and reflected on what it meant to be married. It had changed so much in the twenty some years that he and Liz had been together.

Luke had learned from his own father that commitment to one's family was the highest of traits a man could attain and Luke took those lessons very seriously. They were never spoken and yet were lived out in even the minutest of details in the home in which Luke grew up.

His father was a learned man, a scholar really, who had translated many prayer books from one language to another. Luke had inherited these books upon his father's death and even though he, himself, couldn't read them, he treasured them nonetheless. Maybe, he often thought, the fact that he couldn't read them added to their mystery. He looked at the letters and marveled at his father's intelligence. *How much did you love your faith that you spent countless hours transcribing these prayers with your own hand?*

Of course that led to the regret that Luke had not spent countless hours with his father, quizzing him on the life he had left in the old country and the hardships he most certainly endured in trying to set up a life for his family in this new country filled with immigrants believing in the "American dream."

Could Luke have ever done the same thing? Probably not. And in that recognition resided Luke's tremendous respect and admiration for his father.

But children will be children and in that way they were all the same. Being a child meant living in a somewhat selfish world where your main concerns were about your life and your well-being. You looked to your parents as having an obligation to care for you and you just assumed they would do these things in the appropriate way. It wasn't until he met Liz that he realized not all families operated under the same guidelines.

Elizabeth's parents had divorced when she was but a toddler and both her mother and father eventually remarried. Her father moved to the west coast and her mother remained in the Midwest. Liz never seemed to belong to either family and that pained Luke to no end.

Her step-mother had run hot and cold as long as Luke had known her, until the last few years of her life when she decided that she no longer needed to put on charades and completely stopped communicating with Liz, Luke, and their children. After her death, Elizabeth's father followed her lead and it had now been years since he spoke to Liz. He didn't even know his own grandchildren and for that Luke felt he could never forgive his father-in-law.

Liz did a better job in this department, relying on her faith to get her through. But Luke knew it was a heavy burden on her heart. She had been given a lot of sorrow and grief in her life and now was looking to mend her heartache.

Luke remembered a ridiculous saying from the 60's, where people often talked of "finding themselves." Luke frequently mocked the absurdity of it and yet realized, as he sat looking out his office window, that it was exactly what his beloved Liz was now doing: finding herself. And Luke said a silent prayer that the God she loved so very much would be leading the way.

Chapter Nineteen

*You kingdoms of the earth, sing to God;
chant the praises of the Lord, who rides the
heights of the ancient heavens, whose voice
is thunder, mighty thunder.*
Psalm 68:33-34

When Beth, Sipporah, and Rachel emerged from The Church of the Holy Sepulchre, they were in complete silence. Rachel had been correct in explaining that the entire experience had a way of transporting you to another place and time.

Beth hadn't noticed another soul inside as she joined Christ in His final agonizing moments on earth. She couldn't even say that she had a renewed understanding of His salvific actions or the Father's agape love to have sent His Son.

It was as if she had never even begun to grasp them before, but only now she could attempt to embrace their meaning. She thought of all the Good Friday services she had attended and knew that they would forever have a new place in her heart.

Beth, known for her inquisitive and, according to her children, often annoying nature was rendered mute by the entire experience. In the same way that one woman cannot truly explain to another the pains of childbirth, one pilgrim could not truly explain to another pilgrim what happens during this encounter. To make such an attempt would completely diminish the event because words could not convey its magnitude.

Sipporah and Rachel honored Beth's silence and the three walked back towards Rachel's car. As they drove away Beth started crying. It was soft and yet deep, coming from within the years of pain and sadness that Beth had masterfully hidden. From Christ there were no secrets and in the safety of His death and resurrection Beth, too, was reborn.

Chapter Twenty

Those who love me I also love, and those
who seek me find me. Proverbs 8:17

Seated at a small café, under a faded canopy, the women ordered dinner. Although Beth didn't seem to have much of an appetite, she knew better than to forgo nourishment. She listened as Rachel and Sipporah ordered a cup of coffee and a falafel plate. When it was her turn she ordered the same.

"I think it would be good for us to check in on Miriam and then we will let you relax tonight in your apartment. I hope you have enjoyed your day today and that you will continue to let us be your companions during the next few days."

Beth appreciated Sipporah's suggestion and wholeheartedly agreed, "That would be a perfect way to end what has been a perfect day. And I welcome any time you give me during my stay here."

Beth still had no conversation within her and sat in silence enjoying her coffee and the sights and sounds of the people bustling past her. Rachel, being sensitive to Beth's need for silence, turned her attention towards the street as well. Soon their meals were before them and each closed her eyes in private prayer.

If such a thing is possible, Beth's mind was completely void of thoughts. She ate her falafel, enjoying its aroma arising from its perfect blend of parsley, cilantro, and cumin. The tahini sauce had just enough garlic and lemon to complement the dish and Beth dipped her small sandwich into the bowl with every bite. The side dish of tabouli, made from freshly cut parsley, minced tomatoes and onions was mixed with wonderful cracked wheat and seasoned with olive oil and lemon juice. The entire plate was a feast for the eyes as well as the palate.

Beth had never been "in the moment" as she was at that very point in time. She thought of Christ's words, *I leave you peace,* and understood, as if for the first time, what this gift was that He was bestowing. She had that peace within her and did not want to move for fear it would quickly become but a fleeting memory.

"It is time for us to go check on Miriam," Rachel announced. "Let us make sure she is not in need of anything."

With that, Sipporah motioned for the server to bring them the check, "This is my treat. It has been my priviledge to spend this day with you, Rachel and I look forward to tomorrow as well."

Rachel asked if Beth had any preferences for the next day's sight seeing but Beth found she had none. She thought of all the planning that had gone into the trip and her list of sights and spots to see. Now, all of a sudden, the list seemed so trite. These weren't tourist attractions, these were moments in her Savior's life and she felt almost ashamed that she had written them on a list as if they were rides at an amusement park. "Why don't you make those decisions," she said to Rachel.

"I will do that," was Rachel's simple response.

They drove back to the apartment complex and Rachel parked as close to the curb as possible without actually being on it. Beth smiled and wondered if it reflected Rachel's driving skills or her lack thereof. It seemed that motorists were a frightening bunch in Israel.

In the elevator Sipporah said, "I know that some of Miriam and David's friends were expected today so that Meir could be assured a minyan again. That was very important to him, to be able to praise God as God has called him to do."

Remembering that a minyan was the gathering of at least ten men to pray, Beth wondered if she would have been able to rise to such an occasion as the Goldfarbs had done, praising God in the midst of their grief. But she also understood their commitment to the Torah and was beginning to see how that impacted every aspect of their lives.

At the Goldfarb door, Rachel quietly turned the knob. She knew it would be unlocked for the friends that were coming and going. As the door swung open, Beth caught sight of the praying minyan, now in progress. Sipporah softly closed the door behind them and they walked to Miriam, sitting alone of the couch. Silence seemed to rule the day as Beth and Sipporah simply sat in chairs that had been placed in a semi-circle around the couch.

Rachel took a seat next to Miriam on the couch and put her hand atop Miriam's folded hands that were sitting on her lap. Miriam looked from one loving face to the next, ending with Beth. Beth's nod and smile gave Miriam the information she was searching for: it had been a blessed day. Miriam's head nodded in response and the women sat together for many minutes, content to allow their spirits console and support one another's. In the background Beth could hear the minyan coming to a close. She felt Meir's hand on her shoulder and stood to hug him.

"Bethula, did you have a good day today?"

"It was wonderful, but please do not ask me about my day now, Meir. You are at the center of our thoughts and prayers." Beth said this with all honesty as she had asked Christ, while she was at The Church of the Holy Sepulchre, to cover Meir and his family in peace. She had an errant thought, *Just as I asked Christ to give His peace to Meir, I, too, received the gift I prayed to give.*

Meir nodded his head in understanding and moved to Rachel and then Sipporah. David had also joined them and Beth decided to allow these good friends to spend time together, "If you don't mind, I will go across the hall now." Beth knew from the look of love that seemed to emanate from the small group of friends, that they understood her need to be by herself and wouldn't take it from her.

Back in her apartment, Beth decided to shower and put on a comfortable pair of pajamas. It wasn't as if she were uncomfortable in her outfit but that she simply felt like padding around the apartment in pajamas, robe, and slippers.

Standing in the shower she felt immersed in baptizing waters and let the stream wash away any remnants of hurt, pain, or unforgiveness she might still have harbored in her heart.

Dressed in a fresh pair of cotton pajamas covered in a pattern of pink bows and ribbons, Beth felt as if she were truly a new child, seeing life with eyes of faith. She walked into the kitchen to make herself a cup of tea and stood, transfixed by the day's events. She wondered if a person could withstand the range of emotions that had been hers in the span of five days. She thought of Ayala and Miriam and Rachel and Sipporah. The sheer diversity of the group took her breath away. *What did God have in mind*, she wondered, for the balance of her trip. *And would she be able to travel back to her family and pick up a life that had grown so cold and vacant in the past few years?*

These questions, that once would have plagued her heart and mind, rested instead in the knowledge that Christ would be at her side, providing her with strength and support in whatever the future held.

Chapter Twenty-One

Happy the people who know you, Lord,
who walk in the radiance of your face.
Psalm 89:16

Beth was awakened by the noise coming from the hall between her apartment and the Goldfarbs. Her bedroom shared a wall with the hall and she was, for the first time, made aware of this fact. She stirred in bed and then listened intently to the rise in pitch and volume of the voices. Getting out of bed, Beth pulled on her robe, stepped into her slippers and made her way to the door. She wasn't sure if she wanted to open it and instead put her ear to it in hopes of catching enough words to figure out the cause for the commotion.

Unable to make heads or tails of what was happening, she finally opened the door. Staring right into a neighbor's face, Beth smiled as if to say, *Is everything all right?* but caught herself as she saw Mitzi crying and being held by two other older women, also wrapped in their robes. One of them looked Beth's way, knowing who Beth was but never having had the pleasure of speaking with her and said, "Mitzi's husband passed away this morning. They are taking him now. We are sorry if we have disturbed you."

"Oh my, please, I am sorry Mitzi," Beth said as she left her door ajar and moved towards Mitzi. Mitzi who had been so kind to her just days before, bringing her food and companionship. How ironic that Mitzi, who had so patiently taught Beth how to say the mourner's greeting, was now hearing it issue from Beth's mouth.

Ayala had told Beth earlier in the week that Mitzi's husband had been quite ill for the past few months; congestive heart failure had been the diagnosis. Everyone in the complex knew that his time was limited and yet no one could imagine life without him was what Ayala had said. Again, how ironic it was that Ayala had actually been saying words that would apply to the emptiness her death had left as well. It seemed clear that a friend's death, whether expected or not, left an emptiness that was impossible to fill.

Maybe that was what God intended, Beth thought. That we all have a role to fill, a part in God's divine plan. And when we do what we were brought forth to do, we have affected certain lives in such a way that we continue to live on in the memories of those people. She knew for certain that Ayala would always live on in her heart and mind. Beth also knew that her life was richer for having known Ayala, if only for a few short days. *Could the same be said for people who had known Beth?* She worried that such a statement could not be said. *Was she doing what God called her forth to do?*

As she was standing in the hall, Rachel and Sipporah appeared at the top of the stairs. Mitzi's neighbors began speaking in Hebrew, undoubtedly telling Rachel and Sipporah the news of Chaim's death. Hearing his name, which Beth had completely forgotten, made the memory of him delivering the bag of food from Mitzi flood Beth's mind.

Rachel and Sipporah discreetly removed themselves from Mitzi and her friends and walked with Beth into her apartment. "I'm sorry I'm not ready," Beth apologized. "For the first time in ages I slept in! I think the week is catching up with me."

"Or you've finally let go of some things that have been on your mind, thus allowing you to sleep," offered Sipporah. Beth knew she was right and gave a silent prayer of gratitude for what the restful sleep undoubtedly did for her emotional and physical well-being.

"Give me twenty minutes and we can start our day," Beth said as she headed towards the bathroom to splash her face with cold water and brush her teeth.

"Don't hurry," insisted Rachel. "Where we are going today has been there for thousands of years. A few extra minutes won't matter!"

Beth laughed and closed the bathroom door. She was a willing participant in whatever Rachel had on today's agenda. She splashed the cold water on her face, applied a moisturizer that also contained a sunscreen, and added a few strokes of mascara for good measure. Although as soon as she applied the mascara she regretted it, thinking that if the day held any more tears, her face would be a streaked mess. Staring at herself in the mirror she saw a woman whose neck and jowl line were a bit weaker than just a year ago but whose eyes still sparkled with the hopes of what a new day could bring.

She opted to leave the mascara on and headed to her bedroom where she pulled on yet another monochromatic outfit, tying the requisite sweater around her neck. She was alternating between pairs of shoes and put on the pair she had worn two days before. Looking at herself in the full length mirror, she simply could not decide how she felt about herself. *Did she like what she saw? Was she ready to let go of her youth? Were the answers somewhere "out there" or were they buried deep inside of her?* Letting out a long stream of air through her mouth, she walked into the living room and announced, "Okay, I'm ready!"

Rachel and Sipporah joined her at the door. As they walked out Rachel informed Beth that today they were going to The Wailing Wall, also called The Western Wall, and that they would also venture to Golgotha and the Garden Tomb.

Beth had enjoyed Rachel's discourse before entering The Holy Sepulchre and asked if Rachel would be kind enough to share information about today's sites. Maybe it was the teacher in Beth, but the information ahead of time had made the experience that much more valuable. Rachel agreed and began with information about The Wailing Wall.

"Let's begin by talking of the two terms used interchangeably for the wall. One is "The Western Wall" while the other is "The Wailing Wall." For non-Jews there seems to be no difference but for Jews and Palestinians there is a tremendous difference. This has been especially true since the many talks and negotiations that the west has tried to have between the two warring factions and how the wall might play a significant role in what land is said to belong to whom."

Beth was, once again, intrigued by the information that Rachel was sharing. She knew that Rachel must have been a favorite professor at the university. She clearly enjoyed disseminating knowledge in an interesting and comprehensive way. Beth found Rachel's talks to be quite valuable.

"The length of the Western Wall is significant. Is it simply the area of the wall traditionally used by Jews for prayer and lamentation, which is less than sixty meters, or does it include the entire western retaining wall of the temple mount, the sacred area in which three faiths stake great claims? The

Palestinians want any settlement to use the shorter length while the Jewish state wants any settlement to reflect the entire length which is almost five hundred meters. You can see that this is a significant difference."

Beth thought of the marketplace and the vibrant life that the Arabs brought to it and received from it. She knew that Ayala had fondly thought of the merchants as friends and Beth was glad to have seen the very human side of the difficult co-existence. Ayala and her favorite merchant had died together from assailants still unknown. Two families had been greatly affected by the tragedy: one Arab, the other Jew.

Sipporah was helping Rachel shed light on the history of the wall. "The Hebrew term *ha-kotel ha-ma'aravi* or "Western Wall" is far older than the term "Wailing Wall." This isn't said to bolster the Jewish argument for the length to be determined in their favor, this is just a fact. As early as the seventh or eighth century, we find the term "Western Wall" as being attributed to Rabbi Acha, himself a fourth-century scholar, when he stated that the Shekinah, which is God's presence in the world and with His people, did not leave the "Western Wall." However, there is some question as to whether Rabbi Acha was speaking of today's Western Wall or was he actually referring to the Temple's destroyed west wall? Up to that point there had been no recorded mention of praying and mourning, as happens today. In fact, in the first few centuries after the destruction of the Temple, Roman authorities would not even allow Jews to enter Jerusalem and so their praying and lamenting actually occurred elsewhere. They stood on the Mount of Olives where from that vantage point they were able to look out over the Temple

Mount. If you think about it, it must have been a much more traumatic sight as their eyes could take in all of the destruction instead of standing at a wall in which their view would have been quite myopic."

Beth agreed with Sipporah's assessment recalling the popular phrase, *You can't see the forest for the trees.* So, in this case seeing the forest would have been more heart wrenching for the Jews than just seeing the trees.

Rachel finished where Sipporah had left off, "This practice has been recorded by an early Church Father named Jerome, who witnessed the Jews on the Mount of Olives on the Ninth of Av, the day of mourning and commemoration of the Temple destruction. Father Jerome watched as the Jews looked down upon the ruins, themselves wailing and crying. Ultimately many scholars conclude that the term "wailing wall" was introduced in the twentieth century after the Turks conquered Jerusalem. Either way it seems to be, sadly, one more point of contention between Palestinian and Jew."

By this time they had parked and Rachel suggested that Beth write out a "kvitlich." She said it was a paper that had a prayer, or prayer request, on it and would be inserted into one of the cracks in the wall. Here she was hand delivering her prayers to the wall that God's presence was said to never leave. It was almost too much to bear. Beth's mind flooded with prayers that ran from the purely selfish to the purely selfless. She thought of praying for her children; that Sophia would know how much Beth loved her and felt blessed to have her as a daughter or that one day all her children would find wonderful spouses, or that her own career would flourish, or that the world would know Christ's love and peace.

Her mind was filled with hopes and dreams for herself, her family, her friends, her neighbors, and the world. *What to ask?* she postulated. *Where to begin?*

In the end her prayer request was simple. She remembered the story of a peasant who went to pray but was unable to read from his prayer book. He was an unlearned man, not scholarly, and felt that whatever words he would offer to God would be inadequate. He chose to simply say the alphabet, out loud, and humbly suggested that God use the letters in His own way, for His own purposes. With that in mind, Beth simply wrote on her kvitlich, *Thy will be done.*

With kvitlich in hand, Beth approached the portion of the wall reserved for women. Interestingly, she had no qualms about the segregation. Nothing could surpass her heightened sense of the divine as she neared the wall.

Beth thought of Pope John Paul's historic trip to the Wailing Wall. She was awed by the realization that millions of people had taken the same trip over the course of hundreds of years. God's presence was surely calling them, just as it was calling her now.

For the second time in as many days, Beth understood the magnificence and splendor of God. She entered into communion with Him and neither heard nor saw anyone else at the wall. Time stood still as Beth rocked and swayed and praised the Creator of all that was, is, and ever shall be. She stood in awe of His glory as she inserted her kvitlich into the wall.

Chapter Twenty-Two

The Lord raises the needy from the dust, lifts the poor from the ash heap, seats them with princes, the princes of the people. Psalm 113:7-8

Beth loved the fact that she felt near starvation as they left the wall. For her, the physical emptiness mirrored her spiritual emptiness and she knew that just as a good meal would satiate the pangs in her stomach, God would fill the void in her heart. She had come to the right place and was humbled by that knowledge.

"We are going to stop and eat before we head to the Garden Tomb and Golgotha," remarked Rachel. Sipporah smiled at Beth, sitting in the back seat. To her surprise, Beth realized she had not shed one tear at the wall and Sipporah's smile indicated that she understood, based upon her own experiences, how Beth's journey was unfolding.

Beth had learned, after the death of her beloved grandmother, that there were five stages of grief: denial, anger, bargaining, depression, and acceptance. Beth was beginning to see that she could apply those same stages to her life over the past few years. At first, in her early forties, she began to feel great denial in how her life seemed to be working out.

In a frustrating, dead-end career, kids arguing and fighting with both her and themselves, and seemingly endless lapses in communication between herself and Luke, she literally would find herself saying such things as, *This can't be my life!* If anything could classify as denial, that was Beth's life at forty-two and forty-three years of age.

Then, denial evolved into anger. As she looked around and surveyed what she felt where the ruins of her existence, she became angry. She screamed at the heavens, *Why is this happening to me? What have I done to deserve children like this? Where did my life go?* It was a terrible time for Beth and to get a handle on things she began bargaining with God. *If I work at becoming a better mother, will you make my kids nicer? More respectful? If I promise to stop bickering with my husband will you bring some joy into my life?*

When she made these feeble attempts and didn't see the results she was hoping for, praying for, bargaining for, she became depressed. She literally let the kids sit on the computer for hours at a time. She simply did not care anymore. Weeks went by when she didn't vacuum or fold clothes. Fatigue settled into her bones. She couldn't make the effort to maintain the family and she stopped putting up a fight with the kids.

Her bag of tricks was empty and no one was giving her a refill. It was in the midst of this depression that she had looked at her calendar and hatched her plan to visit the Holy Land. She wondered now if it was divinely inspired as she could literally feel herself moving into the last stage, which was acceptance. But a peaceful acceptance versus a resigned, defeated acceptance. She could feel her heart and soul saying, *With You at my side, I'm ready now for whatever comes.*

There was no panacea for what ailed Beth's life, no quick cures or remedies. Beth was starting to see that life was more like a marathon where there were times you were ahead and times you were behind. Making it to the finish line, so to speak, committed to your goals was what mattered. Beth was starting to see her life with faith filled eyes and like a volcano rumbling deep within, she just knew that an outpouring of peace and tranquility was soon behind.

Rachel opted for a typical "American" restaurant even though Beth could have easily eaten another falafel plate. Seated inside, in a blue vinyl covered booth, Sipporah said, "We thought you might like a good old-fashioned hamburger today!"

Beth would have never considered making her friends feel awkward and agreed that a hamburger sounded perfect. As Beth watched Rachel and Sipporah eat their burgers and fries, she wondered who really wanted a burger!

Getting back into Rachel's car, it was a fairly short trip to their destination. They parked near the Damascus Gate of the Old City and walked up Nablus Road to the beautifully manicured area that very much reminded Beth of the English country gardens she had seen in some of her favorite movies. The silence and simplicity of the garden were in stark contrast to the hustle and bustle of East Jerusalem and the ornate furnishings within the Holy Sepulchre.

Both, however, provided the pilgrim with an opportunity to transcend time and space. There were brochures in languages that she couldn't identify, speaking to the nationalities around the world that called Christ, "Lord." Beth contemplated the realization of the sheer magnitude of people who chose to make this journey and put a physical experience to their Gospel studies.

She picked up a brochure and was reading about Charles Gordon's theory, offered in 1883, which stated that this location was the actual spot referred to in the Gospel of Mark as the 'place of the skull.'

Apparently Gordon, a British general having spent many months in Jerusalem, was looking out of his window and was amazed when he noticed the rock formations that literally looked like a skull. Gordon became convinced that what he was looking at was, literally, 'the place of the skull.'

Many people joined in Gordon's enthusiastic discovery and a fundraising campaign ensued. Its goal was to purchase land adjacent to the formation. By that time, late in the nineteenth century, a rock-cut tomb, various water or wine cisterns, and a wine press had already been excavated. Their cause, and enthusiasm, was bolstered by these finds.

According to the New Testament, Joseph of Arimathea, a wealthy citizen, provided the tomb in which Christ was buried. Although the site seemed to have all the elements to make it a likely place for Jesus' death and burial, more recent research indicated the tomb was actually too old to be Christ's, as His was freshly cut at His death.

Regardless of the conflicting information, Beth felt that the garden provided a wonderful setting in which to contemplate Christ's sacrifice. It was late afternoon and Beth noticed different groups of people gathering in the garden. They weren't like the guided group tours that were also roaming about, enjoying time on the benches and privately sharing their thoughts and prayers with God. Soon these groups had assembled themselves into cohesive units, with some lighting incense and others lost in their own thoughts. Then, as if choirs of angels from heaven had made themselves known, the groups began singing the most melodic chants Beth had ever heard. Taking turns, they praised God and lifted their voices to His throne.

Beth remembered the song that Judge Deborah sang after the Israelite victory over the Canaanites and easily slipped through the cracks of time. Her heart was filled with the edicts of Psalm 100, *Shout for joy to the Lord, all the earth. Worship the Lord with gladness; come before him with joyful songs.* And once again she began humming.

Chapter Twenty-Three

*All the ways of a man may be right in
his own eyes, but it is the Lord who
proves hearts. Proverbs 21:2*

All three women agreed that they would get together the next morning and attend Chaim's funeral. From there they would spend time at Miriam's apartment and then simply walk the marketplace for Beth to pick up some groceries. Beth welcomed the idea of spending more time with her friends and felt thankful for the opportunity to do a mitzvah by attending the funeral. She now embraced the fact that what some would call an imposition; others would call a good deed. It was becoming her way of thinking and she found a deep sense of serenity in its acquisition.

"Okay, I'll see you tomorrow," Beth said as she closed Rachel's car door. Sipporah, sitting in the front seat next to Rachel, smiled out the window and waved good-by. Beth turned towards the apartment complex and heard the honking and beeping of passerbys as Rachel maneuvered her way back into traffic. Smiling, Beth opened the door.

Beth considered checking in on Miriam before entering her own apartment and then changed her mind. She was tired and knew she wouldn't be good company. Besides, tomorrow's plan was in place and Beth would have a much better visit when she was rested and her mind was clearer. Right now she wanted to sit in silence and let the day's sights and sounds take root in every cell of her mind and body. With that goal in mind, Beth decided to fill the tub. She had noticed some crystal decanters of bath beads alongside the bars of soap in the cupboard and could already feel the warm water enveloping her body.

Once inside Beth knew she needed to make a call to Luke. The only real question was if it should be before her bath or after. She decided that after her bath was a better choice. She made her way to the bedroom to get one of her clean loungewear outfits and then to the bathroom to fill the tub. She found the bath beads and probably poured in more than was necessary. She gave in to her indulgent feelings as she watched the bubbles rise and fill the tub, the sweet scent of gardenia filled the air. Undressed, she slowly immersed herself into the water. She had purposely made the temperature hotter than normal with the expectation of spending a good amount of time laying in the tub and letting the memories of the day soak into her very being.

In the tub Beth could feel the odd combination of exhaustion and elation in her body. It was difficult to believe that all she had experienced had happened in less than a week's time. She thought of Ayala and the Goldfarbs. She wondered what sort of accident or tragedy Miriam had experienced that had drawn Miriam and Ayala even closer together in the past few months.

Beth wondered what Luke was doing and how her boys were faring in her absence. She thought of Sophia's demanding school schedule and had to admire her daughter. Sophia was bound and determined to attend the same east coast college that Luke attended and knew what would be required. Sophia's mind, like Luke's, was methodical and pragmatic. Both of them very much unlike Beth, who was more emotional and temperamental. Sophia wanted to study business and finance, ultimately practicing on Wall Street. Beth envied her daughter's convictions and did her best to instill in her daughter a sense of morality and perseverance. Luke, too, admired Sophia, no doubt seeing himself some thirty years younger.

Sophia had made Luke promise not to use his alumni connections when she applied. She wanted to know that she earned her prestigious spot all on her own. While Luke agreed to Sophia's request, Beth wondered about his sincerity. Beth knew that Luke's heart would surely be broken if Sophia's college dreams weren't realized. No one seemed to think of Beth's heart being broken at the thought of her daughter moving hundreds of miles away. Beth decided to let go of those thoughts and concentrated on her bath.

As her mind and body relaxed more in the heat of the gardenia scented tub, Beth could almost hear the chants from Skull Hill and smell the incense. She could see the different denominations taking turns with their hymns and songs and knew that this was how Christ must have hoped the world would live while awaiting His return.

Thinking of the temple mount, Beth tried to imagine the depth of faith Abraham must have had to follow God's request to sacrifice Isaac. Of course it didn't happen, but still Beth had always struggled with the notion that Abraham moved forward as if he *would* sacrifice his own son. Beth had shared her great effort to understand this with Rachel and felt that what she had subsequently revealed to Beth was quite invaluable.

As Rachel explained to Beth, the story of Abraham and Isaac is called, in most Jewish literature, The Binding of Isaac. As the explanation goes, the binding was both a physical binding as well as a spiritual binding. As we know, Isaac was physically bound to the altar but like so many things in life, that was only the surface, or visible, aspect of the story.

Rachel assured Beth that Jewish scholars believe that God reveals Himself in the deeper, more hidden, covert messages of the overt chronicles in the Torah. This meant that while Isaac was literally bound at the altar, so was the realization that when we bind our own self-serving interests and are willing to make painful sacrifices, we are ultimately setting ourselves free.

The bath water was getting cold and as Beth got up to dry off and get dressed she asked herself, *What self-serving interests do I need to bind at the altar?*

Looking in the mirror she realized that the five stages of grief also applied to her physical aging. At first there was denial that her body was getting a bit saggy here and there. Then there was anger that her body could betray her so quickly, so easily.

Following anger was Elizabeth's bargaining in which she hoped that *if* she exercised and ate right *then* her body would show signs of firmness and verve. Depression soon followed as she realized that no amount of exercise was going to stop all the signs of aging. And, like all else, here she was trying to enter the final stage of accepting what was happening to her body.

She had heard all of the arguments against the five stages and yet felt that they best captured her own struggles in so many ways. But for Elizabeth, the last stage was really where she met Christ because it was with Him that she could accept all that life had dealt her, all that life held. And in that way, the stages made perfect sense because they were natural transitions that the Lord seemed to allow her to experience so that she could move into a very personal relationship with Christ.

Chapter Twenty-Four

*When one finds a worthy wife, her value
is far beyond pearls. Her husband,
entrusting his heart to her, has an
unfailing prize. Proverbs 31:10-11*

It was early afternoon when Meghan, Luke's secretary, put Liz's call through. Luke hadn't answered his private office phone which meant he was out in the building. Meghan could page him, wherever he was at.

Liz knew that the boys had the day off from school because of conferences and that Luke was bringing them to work. They liked to play at the computers in his conference room and he enjoyed their enthusiasm. It would be an even shorter day for Luke as he wouldn't want the boys to become restless on his watch. Sophia would be at the library, using the day to search for college scholarships. She knew that Luke and Liz had long ago put money aside for her college education but prided herself on doing things on her own terms. Liz fully believed that Sophia would come up with enough scholarship money to pay for a lion's share of her own tuition.

"Liz! Is everything okay?" were Luke's first words. Although a bit annoyed by them, Liz understood that they were justifiable after the last conversation, in which she had to tell Luke about the explosion and Ayala's death,

"Yes, I'm fine. Everyone is fine. How are you and the boys? Sophia? Have you spoken with Michael?" Liz decided Luke did not need to know about Chaim's death.

"Good. Actually we are doing quite well. I'm sure the boys will tell you that they are both bothered by my early arrival home each day and a bit pleased. You know how that goes. Mike has been busy with a paper he has to write for an English class. He seems to really like his small group discussion leader, so that's a real plus in his accomplishing the work for class. Sophia has been busy working on scholarships."

Liz knew exactly what it was like to have those mixed emotions that Luke was referring to. She had them towards just about everything lately; from her kids to her job to her looks to her marriage. "Yes, I sure know how that goes," She agreed. "And I figured Sophia would be spending time looking for scholarships. She is something!"

"Yes, she is. They all are, actually. And I'm delighted at Mike's turnaround. He's really opened up when we talk and seems so willing to share what's going on at college. Maybe he just needed the distance between us and him. Whatever it is, I'm grateful!"

Liz shared her agreement with Luke before he continued, "So, tell me about your sight seeing? Have you been to the Wailing Wall yet? How about the church you wanted to go to?"

Luke's interest seemed sincere and Liz was quite grateful. She shared some of the highlights of each venture with him but kept some of her personal epiphanies to herself. They just felt very private and like a child with a new toy, she did not want to share.

She then spoke to Joseph and Sammy for a few minutes. Although each conversation was less than ground-breaking, she could feel that they simply loved her and wanted her home. They even spoke of

Sophia's missing Liz. This was yet another epiphany for Liz to put in her back pocket.

When the boys were younger they tended to be more emotional, like Liz. Today she could sense their pragmatic side taking over. Like Luke, they were being neither too talkative nor too emotional, factually stating their love for her. She often missed having no allies with whom to jump up and down or get teary eyed. She would have to make do with her monosyllabic brood.

Sammy gave the phone back to his dad. "Well, we were just heading out for a late lunch, or early dinner, depending on how you look at it. How about you. What have you been eating?"

"Actually, I've probably lost a few pounds because I haven't been eating too many sweets, now that you ask! But I've been enjoying a lot of the native dishes, in particular falafel, tabouli, compote, and chicken soup. It has been delicious, really." ·

"My favorites," Luke interjected and Liz could tell that all the talk of food was making his stomach growl.

"Okay, you need to go feed my children!" she jokingly said.

"Yeah, you're right. We better get going. Liz?"

"Yeah?"

"I love you," Luke said quietly, without grandeur.

Taken aback, Liz said after a few seconds of silence, "Give the kids a hug for me and make sure they eat well. I'll call in a few days." Then she hung up the phone, dismayed at her inability to respond to Luke's proclamation. *Do I love him anymore?* she asked herself as she walked into the living room. *Do I love him?*

Liz had put her reading book on the table by the chair with the intent of digging in tonight. Picking up her reading glasses, she made herself comfortable. Half listening to the traffic noises working their way through her opened window, she began reading. Slowly, the traffic faded as evening made its appearance and everyone headed home. By midnight, she had read a dozen chapters and closed the book. It was as good as she had hoped, and she knew she would make time to finish it over the next few nights. Switching off the lamp, Liz walked towards the bedroom. Hanging her robe on the hook on the back of the door, she stepped out of her slippers and pulled the sheets back. Laying down she thought of Luke's words, *I love you.*

"I love you, too, Luke. I love you, too," Liz said to no one in particular.

Chapter Twenty-Five

*Now that I am old and gray, do not
forsake me, God, That I may proclaim
your might to all generations yet to come.*
Psalm 71:18

The next four days of Beth's vacation
continued to be a myriad of experiences. It was now
the middle of her second week in Israel and she had
but a few precious days left before returning home.
She spent time at Chaim's funeral, more time with
Meir, David, and Miriam, and attended church with
Rachel. Rachel called herself a Messianic Jew and
had given Beth a wealth of intriguing information.
Although Rachel's family was quite unhappy with the
evolution of her faith, Rachel maintained her
commitment to its doctrine: that Jesus was indeed
the Messiah that Jewish people awaited.

Beth could see how this would be offensive to
Rachel's parents but also admitted that it was quite
appealing in that it embraced the Jewish roots of the
Christian faith. This had always been Beth's passion
and she felt that the Lord's hand was in her meeting
Rachel. She questioned Rachel endlessly and then
asked to attend a service with Rachel over the
weekend. Rachel gave Beth some literature to read
after the service and Beth was astounded at the
intricate use of Scripture in supporting the Messianic
Jewish position. That was Sunday and Beth had
spent the entire evening reading.

The literature stated that Messianic Jews
believed that the bible included the Holy Scriptures
as well as the New Testament, which they called B'rit
Hadasha, and was the infallible and authoritative

word of God. They believed in its divine inspiration and embraced it as the ultimate source of guidance in all matters of faith.

Rachel gave Beth a bible to use while she read through the literature and Beth looked up such verses as Deuteronomy 6:4-9 which said, *Hear, O Israel! The Lord is our God, the Lord alone! Therefore, you shall love the Lord, your God, with all your heart, and with all your soul, and with all your strength. Take to heart these words which I enjoin on you today. Drill them into your children. Speak of them at home and abroad, whether you are busy or at rest. Bind them at your wrist as a sign and let them be as a pendant on your forehead. Write them on the doorposts of your houses and on your gates.*

Beth finished reading the verse and thought of the men at the wailing wall, wearing their tefillin, clearly following this command. Tefillin are the straps that the men wore around their arms and head that had words from the Torah written upon them.

Beth then looked at the doorpost of her bedroom door and knew that the mezuzah, a small ornate metal container with the Lord's Commandments inside, was also adhering to this passage. Beth put the bible aside and picked up the brochure again. She saw many passages sited for the support of God's Word as authoritative, infallible, and the only place to look for real guidance.

Beth had learned from David and Miriam that all Jews begin their day with the Shema. This was also taken from Deuteronomy and was a proclamation that said, *Hear, O Israel, the Lord our God, the Lord is one.* As Beth read the brochure she saw that the Shema was also a foundation for the Messianic Jewish faith where they understood that this one true God existed in three persons: Father, Son, and Holy Spirit. The brochure referenced Romans 8:14-17 and Beth turned there in the bible.

After Beth finished reading Romans she turned her attention back to the brochure. Next it explained their belief in God as the Father, or Abba. Beth almost skipped over this as it seemed a given until it struck her that in using the term 'Abba,' it was safe to assume that there was a child and that child was Jesus! The revelation energized Beth and she looked up many of the verses sited: John 6:27b; I Corinthians 1:3; Gal. 1:1; Rev. 3:5, 21; Jeremiah. 3:4, 19; 31:9; Mal. 1:6; Matt. 6:9, 32; Luke 10:21-22; John 1:14; 4:23; 5:17-26; 6:28-46.

By that time it was late afternoon and Beth had no plans for the evening. She had assured Rachel and Sipporah that she enjoyed some of the quiet evenings at home. Beth went to the refrigerator and made herself another light dinner. The trip had been filled with so many blessings, not the least having been her drastically altered eating habits. She hadn't had a bag of chips or a candy bar or a piece of cake since she had been in Israel.

Although her waist wasn't returning to its pre-maternity size, she could finally feel a bit of room in her clothes and that little bit of success urged her on. Her appetite for sweets and salts was practically gone. Beth enjoyed her dinner on the balcony and felt a pang of regret that she would soon be leaving. She had made friends, seen sights, and had experiences that would stay with her forever. *Would she ever come back? Only God knew.*

Finishing her meal, she washed her dish and silverware and went to the end table to pick up the brochure. She was interested in reading how the Messianic Jews reconciled Jesus as the Son. He was called HaBen and there were countless verses to support this: Psalm 2; Proverbs. 30:4-6; Luke 12:35-37; John 1:29-34, 49; 3:14-18. Most intriguing to Beth was their acceptance of Mary as the virgin who bore Christ and the clear call to worship Him as God. There was no middle ground. He wasn't an exalted prophet, He was Yeshua, Salvation. In black and white the brochure staked the claim that Christ was the Messiah of Israel, again indicating numerous verses to support this truth.

Beth then turned her attention to the information regarding God as the Holy Spirit, or what they called Ruach HaKodesh. Beth had participated in a study group years before where a lot of the work had been done in understanding 'Ruach.' Here it was used as the 'Spirit of God' but Beth also recalled learning how it was God's breath, speaking the world into being, or something like that. She was frustrated with herself that she couldn't clearly recall everything they had talked about during that study group.

Beth shook off her irritation and continued reading about man being created in God's image and that he fell due to his own disobedience. This, then, led to all men being born with a sinful nature. She had to wholeheartedly agree as she thought of her own transgressions in her marriage and elsewhere. She heard David talking about sins and she realized that while she would have, up until that point, put her sins in a 'lesser' category, that wasn't always the way that Adonai would view them.

Beth put the brochure down, took off her reading glasses and thought of her marriage. She decided to make herself a cup of tea and put on the tea kettle. Selecting a new flavor, raspberry, she put the tea bag in her cup and waited for the water to

come to a boil. Soon the kettle was whistling and
Beth watched as the hot water, pouring over the tea
bag, turned to a reddish-purple color in her cup.
Beth stirred absentmindedly for a few minutes and
then, using the back of a spoon, she squeezed the bag
against the side of the cup. Taking the dehydrated
bag out of the water, she walked over to the waste
basket to throw away the tea bag. Then, cup in hand,
she headed back towards what had become her
favorite chair.

As she continued reading the Messianic
brochure, she found great comfort in the words of
Ephesians 2:8-9, *For by grace you have been saved
through faith, and this is not from you; it is the gift of
God; it is not from works, so no one may boast.*
Messianic Jews also believed in the resurrection and
judgment with the redeemed sharing in everlasting
life and the lost forever separated from God.

On that note, Beth decided to put everything
away for the night and go to bed. She slept soundly
and when she awoke Monday morning, resumed her
reading. By noon Beth had read more scripture
verses than she had over the course of the previous
year. From the promise of the second coming as
revealed in 1 Thessalonians as well as in John and 1
Corinthians, to the spiritual redemption of Israel as
revealed in Romans and Hebrews, Beth was
transfixed. With every word she read, she was
renewed.

When Beth read the full prophecy that the
Messiah's return shall indeed be in Zion she thought
of Suleiman's attempt to seal the gate in the Western
Wall to prevent just that! Beth found herself
frightened at the prospect of the second coming. *How
would she be judged?* she wondered. *Was her
relationship with Christ real or was it wishful*

thinking that there was more to life than this fleeting earthly existence?

Beth finished the brochure by reading their statement of faith, replete with bible verses to support the statement.

We recognize that Jewish people (physical descendants of Abraham through Isaac and Jacob, whether through the mother's or the father's blood-line) who place their faith in Israel's Messiah, Yeshua, continue to be Jewish according to the Scriptures (Rom. 2:28-29). Gentiles who place their faith in Yeshua, are "grafted into" the Jewish olive tree of faith (Rom. 11:17-25) becoming spiritual sons and daughters of Abraham (Gal. 3:28-29).

We observe and celebrate the Jewish Holy Days given by God to Israel, with their fulfillment in and through the Messiah Yeshua. We believe that true "Biblical Judaism," the faith of first century believers, which we seek to practice, acknowledges the continuity of faith in the one true God, revealed throughout the Scriptures, and ultimately manifested in God's Son, Yeshua the Messiah. We believe that salvation has always been "by faith," and that works of law, or righteous acts, have never saved anyone (Gen. 15:6; Rom. 2-6; Eph. 2:8-9; Heb. 11:6, 39).

We acknowledge that the New Covenant body of believers is composed of both Jews and Gentiles who have received Yeshua the Messiah as the Promised Redeemer. The "middle wall of partition" has been broken down and now we worship the God of Israel together (I Corinthians. 12:13; Eph. 2:13-14).

After finishing the brochure, Beth found herself in a contemplative mood and decided to take a stroll around the neighborhood. She pulled on a pair of jeans and grabbed her all-purpose sweater. It was late Monday afternoon and the next day she was to be spending with Miriam, Rachel, and Sipporah. Shivah was over and Miriam was looking forward to getting together with "the girls." Beth had thoroughly enjoyed her day roaming around the apartment, reading, and relaxing.

Tomorrow and Wednesday would hold a few more sights, a few more conversations, and the week would finish on Thursday evening, when she would head back home. Rachel and Miriam would be driving Beth to the airport; Sipporah had a meeting with her professor for a few last minute edits on her thesis. The next few days would also be filled with 'good-byes' as she would not see Sipporah after tomorrow. David, too, was leaving for a sabbatical before he began his education as a rabbi.

Beth's heart was already aching, torn between her new found friends and her love of the Holy Land and her need to get back to her own life in the states. She was a wife and a mother, a teacher and a friend. She strolled around the neighborhood, taking in every last detail in case she was never to make it back. She didn't want to forget even the minutest of details from this magnificent trip.

Chapter Twenty-Six

*Wash away all my guilt; from my sin
cleanse me. Psalm 51:4*

Luke was eagerly anticipating Liz's return, as
were the kids. To his surprise, even Michael had
called home to see how things were going with her.
Miracles, Luke concluded, were still happening!

Sitting in the comfort of his favorite chair,
Luke replayed his conversations with Liz over the
past two weeks. There had been only a handful but
he felt that each one was significant. At first both he
and Liz were hesitant to utter any words of
endearment. Each was somehow sizing up the
situation as well as his or her own feelings. Therapy
had been step one but step two was more of an
internal "coming to terms" with what had been, what
was, and what could possibly be.

Neither Luke nor his wife were dreamers and
had to decide if this marriage was going to work on
its own terms or if either was interested in throwing
in the towel. Luke was more likely to accept the
status quo whereas Liz was looking for some serious
change. He felt that although there were things she
was looking for from him, the bigger question was
simply if she were willing, or able, to move into a
place of peaceful acceptance. While he didn't believe,
not for one minute, that this was "selling out," he
knew that Liz harbored those fears.

He could see it in her eyes, hear it in her
arguments, and feel it in their relationship. For Liz,
accepting life as it had turned out felt like she was
"settling." She had thrown around those phrases for

a few years now: settling, selling out. Each had been spewed out as if poison. Luke knew there was no convincing Liz that life just had a way, like an old house, of settling. He wanted her to understand, though, that the settling of a foundation meant that the creaks and groans had all been worked out. Yes, there seemed to be more energy when you never knew what to expect, but things shouldn't stay that way.

Luke thought of a verse he heard in church and wrote it down. He wanted to share it with her but knew the time had to be right. He knew that the words were so applicable to their marriage that his confidence in sharing them with Liz was bolstered. Getting up from the chair, Luke made the decision to go to the store and find a greeting card for Liz that captured how he felt and hoped she still felt as well.

If nothing else, he would find a nice card that was blank inside and write his own sentiments. A little annoyed with himself, he realized that the last time he had sat down and really put his heart in what he wanted to say was when he had engraved their wedding bands with the words, *Our Destiny Awaits.*

This wasn't to say that he hadn't bought cards and flowers over the years, but he could see Liz's point that things had definitely changed over their lifetime together. He now wanted to put them back on track. He knew he had more to give than he had given in a long time. It became imperative for him to put the long term effort into this marriage that he had put into his company.

Chapter Twenty-Seven

*I will live for the Lord; my descendants
will serve you. Psalm 22:31*

The last two days of Elizabeth's trip were wonderful. On Tuesday, all four women spent their last day together in the beautiful hills and valleys by the Sea of Galilee. It was in Northern Israel and filled with man-made and natural wonders. One of their stops was in the city of Safed. Rachel explained that during the middle ages it became a haven for Spanish Jews as a result of the Inquisition. "Many people consider this to be the most peaceful of settings that exist in the world."

Beth had to agree with Rachel, as did Miriam and Sipporah. The mountaintop city and view was breathtaking. Everywhere they looked were streams running through the mountains, determinedly making their way to the sea.

"The Jews of Galilee used Mt. Arbel as a stronghold during their fighting with the Romans in the first century. But let's not think of these things today!" Sipporah said, wanting to steer their last day together in a completely different direction than the endless fighting that seemed to be part of man's inherent nature. "Let's rent a kayak and ride down the Jordan River!"

Beth almost fell over at Sipporah's suggestion. She had never been fond of boats and the only images she could conjure up regarding kayaking or rafting had to do with turbulent whitewater waves throwing all occupants into a rabid stream just waiting to plunge everyone to their death. Beth remained quiet to better hear all the other protests. To her dismay, everyone thought rafting or kayaking was a great idea and they were apparently on their way to some undisclosed kayak rental place with Beth trailing behind. *Wouldn't that be something if this was how I lost my life?* Beth murmured to herself. Of all of Luke's concerns, both spoken and not, Beth could bet on the fact that Luke never considered Beth would step foot in a kayak.

Within minutes they were gearing up for a boat ride and Beth felt that the whole thing had been planned. She knew she was right as Sipporah spoke, "I hope you won't find us too pushy but we wanted to spend our last day together doing something a bit out of the ordinary so that when you thought of the Holy Land you thought of the times of Christ but also of today. Of all the things He has done for you, He has also brought you to us and made us feel as if we have always known you."

Beth began crying and all four women hugged in one of those big, dramatic group hugs that are so often made fun of on television. But nothing was more appropriate, more fitting, than for these four friends to create a circle and laugh and cry for a few precious minutes.

"Ladies, let me just check your gear and you can get into the quad-kayak," instructed their guide. Beth was relieved that they weren't being left to their own devices and was the second to board. The boat was bigger than she had imagined. She looked around and saw assorted kayaks and canoes, all holding multiple occupants. Everyone seemed to be enjoying themselves and she decided to have fun as well.

She shared a bench with Rachel. They looked at each other and giggled. Beth asked, "Have you done this before?"

"Many times. It is truly a fun experience. One you will never forget. We have all done this together, quite a few times. Now, we will always be able to remember you as part of our kayaking stories!"

Once they were in, the guide instructed them on the proper principles of leaning and ducking but mostly stressed that he would be able to handle what was ahead and that they should all enjoy the ride. Beth was relieved because by the time he gave the third instruction she had already forgotten what the first one was. Apparently even time in the Holy Land couldn't erase the symptoms of menopause! She laughed and Miriam asked her what was so funny. "Just an inside joke," was Beth's response and the girls nodded in agreement, apparently all understanding that inside jokes were best left, well, inside. They smiled as the kayak took its place in the river.

The trip down the Jordan River was just one more highlight in a vacation filled with unforgettable experiences. Beth got soaked on more than one occasion and could not stop laughing. Soon, all four women were laughing at nothing in particular. If a feeling, a moment in time, could be a magical elixir, then Beth and Miriam and Rachel and Sipporah had their fair share that afternoon. And if laugher truly is good medicine, then each woman stood up from the kayak healthier than when she entered.

They made their way back to the car and began their trip home. The smiles on their faces reflecting the beauty of their day together. Driving home they each simply took in the sights of men and women and children busy with their life's activities.

Dropping off Sipporah, Beth got out of the car
to give her a hug. "Thank you for all your time.
Please keep me informed about your life and your
studies and I will do the same."

Hugging Beth, Sipporah responded in kind.
Then they pulled away from each other and smiled.
Beth got back into Rachel's car and they drove away.
As much as Beth wanted to look back, she actually
couldn't. Her throat ached with the tears that
threatened to erupt. Looking back at Sipporah would
have unleashed emotions that Beth was afraid were
far bigger than just their good-byes.

Rachel parked her car in the street in front of
the apartment complex. They had eaten a late lunch
and all had agreed that dinner was of no interest.
Miriam, Beth, and Rachel would be spending
Wednesday together. Thursday, Beth was returning
home. Her short trip was coming to an end. And yet,
in a very wonderful way, Beth felt as if she had been
in Israel for months. She loved the familiar sights
and sounds and realized that in her two brief weeks
she had known the tragedy and triumph that made
up the Holy Land.

Closing the car door, Beth said to Rachel,
"Okay. We'll see you tomorrow morning?"

"Around ten?" Rachel asked in agreement.

"Perfect," responded Miriam. They had all
found that mid-morning gave everyone a chance to
get their day off without a rush and thus enjoy it
more fully.

Rachel pulled the car out into traffic with the
requisite honking and maneuvering. Beth and
Miriam headed up the stairs in silence. They always
alternated between the elevator and stairs, somehow
remaining in sync with their steps, whichever route
they were taking. Miriam broke the silence when she

asked Beth, "Do you want to stop by to say good-bye to David?"

Beth had not anticipated leaving Israel to be an emotional venture and yet that was exactly what it had developed into. She had come to dearly care for the Goldfarbs and Rachel and Sipporah and now had to say good-bye, not knowing if she would ever see them again. It was an odd feeling, reminiscent of when she was a young girl and her father would be in town on business. He would take Beth to dinner and then drive her home. Inevitably he was catching a plane to some other city, some other state, forever building his business for himself and his wife and their daughters. But never Beth. She was never a priority. She saw him now and again and each time was like ripping the scar off her heart, only to have her build it back up again.

It was always the same. Her father would drop her off and she would walk to her front door. The ache that she had in her throat when saying good-bye to Sipporah was the ache in her throat back then, making it almost impossible for her to swallow. She would never forget the physical pain she would feel as her heart raced and her tears became suffocating. She never knew if she would see her father again. Would he be back or would he be gone forever? If it wasn't for his business in town, she now knew she never would have seen him. Period. *Would that have been better?* She would never know.

As it was, each time she saw him she experienced the identical pain. It was really too much for a young girl to bear and now as a mother she would never be able to stand the idea of her children withstanding such emotional turmoil.

"Yes, I would like to say good-bye to David," was Beth's quiet reply.

Miriam opened the door to her apartment and Beth walked inside. *Was it just a dozen days ago that I walked in here for the first time?* Beth couldn't believe how much two weeks could hold. She had been living in such a way that it seemed like her life held nothing new and here she was, two weeks in Israel, and she had more experiences than the past five years of her life.

"Please, sit down. I'll put on a pot of tea. It will be nice to have some fruit and cheese and visit together."

Beth agreed and made her way to the couch. The window was open and the breeze was refreshing. David walked into the room from the small hallway and smiled as he saw Beth. "Shalom! What a pleasant surprise."

Beth returned David's warm smile and imagined all the families he would counsel, guide, and know as a rabbi. Although most rabbis agree that their decision is one of great contemplation and prayer, that they are not "called" in the way that most Christians consider their pastors or priests "called" to the religious life, there had to be something along those lines nonetheless. Beth figured that the reality for both was probably somewhere in the middle. God did a little calling and the recipient did a little praying, and before long they came to an understanding of how to best glorify God's kingdom here on earth.

"Do you want any help, Miriam?" David called towards the kitchen.

"No, I'm fine. Where's abba?"

"He went out with some friends. I believe they are visiting and enjoying one another's company."

David explained to Beth that after Shivah it was a responsibility of someone close to the family to encourage them to take up the things of life: going out again and so on. Beth knew that Meir would have been surrounded by such people who cared for his well being and could easily say that Ayala would have wanted him to enjoy his days as well. She was truly special.

Beth stayed for about an hour during which time she and Miriam and David exchanged pleasantries. It was an easy conversation with Beth recounting their day's kayaking experience. David laughed heartily as Miriam pantomimed the four women doing their best to help the guide keep the kayak upright.

All in all, David admitted, it seemed to have been a perfect ending for Beth's vacation. At his words, her heart leapt with the knowledge that when she arrived, David had a mother and now as she was departing, he did not. She shook her head in dismay and David asked what she was thinking about. In all honesty she replied, "Your mother."

David and Miriam exchanged glances and Miriam spoke up, "Beth, my father and David and I have something we would like you to have."

Beth looked from Miriam's face to David's and then back to Miriam's. David left the room and returned with a container the size of an old-fashioned hat box. He handed it to Beth who reached up her arms to receive it.

She placed it on her lap and looked at them again. "I don't know what to say. This is very kind and, of course, I have nothing to give you but my gratitude for your graciousness, kindness, and friendship." Tears welled up in Beth's eyes as she lifted the lid. Inside, packed in blue and white tissue paper was a ceramic tea set. Beth recognized it immediately. It was the tea service with which Ayala had served Beth on Beth's first night in Israel. Its porcelain exterior beautifully decorated with roses and vines, hand painted, Ayala had said when Beth originally complimented it.

When Beth looked at David and Miriam, they, too, were crying. David spoke in such a soft voice that Beth had to strain to hear him, "Beth, as you know, my mother was a wonderful woman. She loved everyone and did her best to make all people feel welcome in her home. She was especially fond of you, Beth, and would have wanted you to have this set."

Beth started to object but David raised his hand to quiet her concerns before he continued, "The interesting thing about this, Beth, was that my mother knew right away she wanted you to have the set. That was why she was going to purchase a new set. She had already told us she wanted you to have this one."

Beth could not breathe upon hearing those words. She looked at Miriam and David and realized that they could have hated her and she never, ever would have blamed them. Groaning, Beth apologized profusely and both the Goldfarb children hugged her.

David comforted her, once again, with his words. "Beth, my father and I have already gone to the home of the Arab merchant who was also killed in the blast. He left behind a wife and four children. Like my mother, his wife is a loving, caring woman who holds no hatred in her heart. We hugged one another because in these deaths, we are more alike than different. Each of our families will somehow go on but will be very different than they were.

Our world is filled with much hate and bloodshed and my mother would never want someone else's hatred to infiltrate her family. And so Beth and I want you to know that you will always be very special to us and that we could never harbor ill feelings towards you because nothing you did was wrong. You brought out our mother's love. How could we hate that?"

Miriam's silence was as powerful as David's words, each contributing to Beth's overwhelming understanding of love and forgiveness.

"We've packed the set in a way that it would probably survive the trip but thought it might be better if we shipped it separately. What do you think?" Miriam asked Beth.

Beth surveyed the tea set and knew that it was as fragile as life itself. "Please, let's ship it separately and pack it with a bit more padding."

"Okay, I'll take this to the postal service tomorrow and you should be getting it in two or three weeks," David said.

Hugging David, Beth said her good-byes and walked across the hall to her apartment. Standing in the Goldfarb doorway, Miriam called out, "I'll see you tomorrow around ten. Sleep well."

Chapter Twenty-Eight

Awake, my soul; awake, lyre and harp! I will wake the dawn. Psalm 57:9

If Miriam's words had been a command, Beth's sub-conscious could not have been more attentive. Beth couldn't remember the last time she had slept so peacefully two nights in a row. It was as if every inch of her body had absorbed David's words about his mother's love and forgiveness and that of the merchant's wife as well. Getting out of bed, Beth walked straight to the bible. She was intent on finding the verse about peace and tranquility and health. Somehow she just knew they were all connected.

Unsuccessful, Beth turned her attention to making a pot of coffee. Over the past two weeks she had come to crave the rich, dark taste and aroma of the coffee her hosts had provided. Once the coffee pot was set up and turned on, Beth made her way to the bathroom. There were a few items drying on the line across the tub and she removed them before she started the shower. As she washed her face and contemplated tomorrow's trip home, she was reminded of Jacob's struggle with an angel of God. Jacob, who wouldn't release the angel until he had given Jacob a blessing, was determined to get his way, what he felt was rightfully his. Beth had those same feelings towards her life. She wanted what was rightfully hers, nothing more but certainly nothing less.

Stepping out of the shower, Beth dried herself and threw on her robe. Walking to the bedroom to get dressed, she thought about the day ahead. Oftentimes Beth got caught up in the small details of life. For instance, here she was, in Israel, and in thirty-six hours she would be in the states. Things like that seemed to always occupy her mind. She often wondered if other people found any fascination in these things.

While she dressed she took the opportunity to begin packing. She reasoned that if she did it in increments, it would be less painful. She was a "slowly-peel-off-the-band-aid" kind of a gal whereas Luke was a "rip-it-off-in-a-millisecond" kind of guy. *Could the two find everlasting peace and happiness?* She really wondered.

Eating a piece of flat bread and some cheese with her morning coffee, Beth heard footsteps in the hall. The day was underway, Beth thought with a heavy heart. She opened the door before Rachel had a chance to knock. Miriam, too, must have heard the footsteps and was in the hall.

"Let me just run and brush my teeth and then I'm good to go," Beth said to them both.

"We'll meet you in the car," was Rachel's reply.

Minutes later, getting into the car, Beth asked about the day's agenda. She was game for anything and knew Rachel would have the perfect plans.

While they drove, Beth tried to fathom what they could do or see that would add to her trip. She felt, in her heart, that it had been more than she could have ever imagined and now she sat filled with a tremendous mix of emotions. She remembered when Sammy had outgrown the stroller. For many years it had been like a useless appendage to Beth. Everywhere she went, the stroller went. As soon as one child grew out of it, another needed it. And then, before she knew it, toddler Sammy was not interested in the comforts of chauffeur service from his mother or even his siblings. No, her youngest wanted to walk with everyone else. At first Beth was elated. *Finally*, she had said to herself.

Then, one day as she was driving home from work, she saw a young mother pushing a stroller. Pedaling along side the stroller was the "big" sister. Beth had guessed the little girl's age to be around three. There was a little sway to the girl's peddling and her pony tails were waving back and forth. Beth, of course, could not remember any of her walks as peaceful as the one she had just witnessed.

Beth mostly remembered Michael or Sophia complaining that she was walking too fast or too far. Then Joseph would begin crying and soon everyone was miserable. But time sweetened her memories and as Beth drove past this mother pushing the stroller she was overcome with melancholy. Melancholy was an odd mixture of sadness and regret mingled with the beauty of a memory of what once was and is no more.

That was exactly how Beth felt today. Melancholy. Of course she couldn't wait to see her children and yet she was realistic enough to know that the aura would rub off rather quickly and within days, maybe even hours, her life would be right back where it was. And that was her dilemma. She had not spent any real time, in Israel, thinking of her hopes and dreams and of what life had become without her permission. Now she was just hours from returning and had no answers.

When she boarded the plane two short weeks prior, she assumed she would have answers. Somewhere in the middle of the Holy Land she expected God to speak to her, clearly and succinctly, so that she could either accept her life or move on.

But He had not spoken to her. Not in so many words, at least. He had touched her heart in ways she couldn't even begin to describe but He had not given her the clear answers she had wanted so very much regarding her marriage and her life.

Rachel pulled into a spot on a street in front of a large apartment complex and put the car in park. Beth looked inquiringly at Miriam who shrugged and smiled. Rachel was already out of the car, obviously full of anticipation for whatever was held in this building.

Beth and Miriam joined Rachel at the front door and followed her into a beautifully marbled foyer with lush green ferns perched atop tall alabaster columns that flanked the sides of the stairs as well as the elevator door.

"Here we are!" Rachel announced.

"Which is where?" Beth asked.

"My home," Rachel answered in an elevated voice. She was barely able to contain her excitement.

"Do we need to pick something up?" was all Beth could think of as she followed both Rachel and Miriam up the stairs.

Not answering, Rachel opened the first door to their left on the second floor. Right away Beth noticed a beautifully set table with crystal water goblets and china that was catching the light from the window. The chairs were upholstered with rollback tops and skirted bottoms. The table was covered in a delicate lace tablecloth. The silverware was ornate with carved handles of silver and gold. As the women approached the table Beth could see that the design on the silverware was of intricately woven tendrils of vine that matched the design on the outer edge of the plates. Everything was beautiful.

"Since you were such a good sport about us hijacking you to go kayaking, we hoped you would also be agreeable to this. We have decided to spend the day together, here in the apartment, just visiting. Sort of like the young girls today have pajama parties! Sharing our heart's desires, life's challenges, dancing around, and giggling along the way. The only thing we won't do is set each other's hair! What do you think?"

Miriam looked at Beth to see her reaction as well as hear her words. Like Ayala, Miriam had a way of knowing things. A sixth sense, really. And Beth knew that if she wasn't agreeable to this day, neither Miriam nor Rachel would have had a problem. They would clear the table and head out the door and enjoy whatever Beth had in mind. "I couldn't think of a better way to spend my last day here! Let the pajama party begin!"

Chapter Twenty-Nine

And not forget the works of God, keeping
his commandments.
Psalm 78:7

The women sat at the table and enjoyed the lavish meal that Rachel and Miriam had gone to great lengths to prepare. There were eggs and fish, fresh fruit, and fresh baked rolls that released steam when they were pulled apart. It was a feast for a queen and they made sure that was how Beth felt.

After they finished their meal, Rachel walked over to a small desk that sat off to the side of the couch. On it was a magenta gift bag with a silver ribbon tying the handles together while also cascading down the sides of the bag. Back at the table, Rachel gave the bag to Beth. "I'm not sure I'm emotionally up to receiving another gift," Beth announced, thinking of Ayala's tea set.

"I only hope this will be as special to you as was the Goldfarb gift. This is actually from me and Sipporah, who is saddened that she could not spend this day with us."

Beth tugged on one end of the ribbon and it easily slipped out of its knot. Pulling the ribbon through the handles, Beth placed it on the table. When she opened the bag she saw two books inside. Intrigued, she looked at Rachel and then at Miriam. Both women smiled as they knew more about Beth than Beth realized. Picking up both books at once, Beth withdrew them from the bag. Each was no larger than the book of Psalms that she had brought with her but had never really had a chance to read.

The first book was leather bound and had a ribbon marker attached to the inside that could be moved and placed on any page that Beth was reading. The cover had an inscription that was in Hebrew. Beth looked up at Rachel who said, "This book has all the names of God. It is very popular among Messianic Jews."

Beth carefully thumbed through the pages. It wasn't a thick book but each page was like a work of art with a heading in Hebrew and then the text in English. Beth put the book on her lap and picked up the second book. It was smaller than the first and was a book about Sarah, Rebekah, and Rachel. Beth was more than intrigued, she was downright anxious to read about these special women. "You already know how much these mean to me and I thank you for these. I will treasure them always!"

The women moved from the table to the living room. The windows were open and Beth enjoyed the sounds of the city below. It was just one more thing that she would miss when she was home. Miriam helped Rachel make a tray with coffee and also brought the remaining breakfast rolls. Beth settled in on a large chair while Rachel and Miriam shared the couch. Miriam tucked her legs up under herself in a way that showed her comfort in her friend's home. Beth had carried the books to the chair and placed them on the end table.

Their conversation continued and they shared some of their innermost feelings. Beth was both comforted and amazed that, no matter where a woman lived, her life was filled with demands and required perseverance and diligence. Neither Rachel nor Miriam had children but seemed to have their hands full with other things that Beth did not. Listening to them, Beth felt that she could never have handled the stress placed upon them in their respective careers. She also wondered how they coped with the loneliness to which they both alluded.

"Why do you think all women have some sense of loneliness? I would have guessed that you were both so fulfilled with your careers and good friends that you wouldn't feel lonely," Beth hoped neither one was offended by her frankness but Rachel did say this was pajama party time.

Miriam, who seemed as knowledgeable as Rachel on so many topics, was the first to answer. "I believe St. Augustine said it best when he said that, and I'm paraphrasing here, we are restless until we rest in the Lord. I have met women from all over the world and am always taken aback by what you just observed. When it comes right down to it, there is a restlessness stirring in each and every one of us. It sends us on our journeys, searching to fill the void, so to speak, in our hearts and in our souls. For many of us it is a physical aching, knowing we are somewhat empty, no matter what our life holds; marriages, careers, children, health, and even prosperity.

None of these things fill that place within us that God has created for His own indwelling. Yes, people try many ways to fill it, to stop the ache, but nothing is able to do the trick. That is because it can only be filled by God Himself. And even then, as St. Augustine had said, we are still somewhat restless because our final destiny is to be with God."

As they continued talking they reflected on their many different friends, family members, neighbors, and co-workers. The common denominator did, indeed, seem to be that regardless of station in life or personal circumstances, all the women they knew, collectively and individually, were in one way or another restless. For many it only became apparent, after certain goals were attained in which the restlessness did not cease, that their need was for something far greater than the earth provided. Their need, each and every one of them, was their Lord.

Like a stream that snakes through hills and valleys on its way to a mighty river, so too, was their conversation. Everything seemed to lead up to the books that had been given to Beth. "Now why does God have more than one name?"

Rachel, who had studied the names of God in great depth, was more than willing to share her knowledge. "Although there is some debate among scholars as to the impetus behind the many names of God, it can be said that all Jews revere His name so completely because they believe it is a revelation of His nature. Thousands of years ago, before scribes would copy His name from one manuscript to the next, they would bathe and pray to be worthy of such an honor!"

Beth was dumbstruck by such an idea. Not because she, too, didn't revere the very nature and essence of God, but because she thought of the carelessness with which people threw around His holy name.

"In fact," Rachel continued, "Judaism avoids uttering God's name outside of temple and the original use in Genesis is without vowels, which leaves current scholars debating whether or not anyone really even knows the correct pronunciation anymore. Although a very common accepted pronunciation is 'Yahweh' which is made up of the Hebrew letters *Yod-Heh-Vav-Heh*. This name is often called 'The Unutterable Name.' Since a name reflects a person's being, and should be treated as respectfully as the person himself, the name for the magnificent and blessed Creator would be beyond uttering for mere man. Of course Christ crosses those barriers for us, and yet the beauty of such worship is undeniable."

Beth picked up her leather book with the names of God revealed on the interior pages, and gently flipped through, admiring each of the names, honoring them as Rachel was suggesting. She had always found great beauty in the Hebrew alphabet and already knew that these books would become her favorites at home. Now, thinking that they held the revered name of God, their importance was beyond compare. Not only did they reveal knowledge about the many different attributes of God and His people, but they were given to her with love and affection.

Beth stopped on the page with the name El Shaddai. Rachel noticed Beth's interest remain on the page and quietly let Beth read that El Shaddai was translated into God Almighty and that this name was in many places throughout Scripture but most interesting to Beth was that it was in the first book of the bible, Genesis, and in the last book of the bible, Revelation.

Beth looked up at Miriam and Rachel and apologized, "I'm sorry! But you can see that this was the perfect gift! I will use my tea service to make myself tea and sit and enjoy these books." Both Miriam and Rachel were honored to have given Beth something that she already envisioned using together. "Please, go on," Beth insisted.

"Well, let's consider the name you were just reading about: Shaddai. Some scholars, and I'm sure regular people like me who are simply interested in learning all they can about God, understand that at the root of Shaddai is a word which also means 'to overpower' or 'to destroy.' Can you see how that is connected to the title 'Almighty,' because it is God Almighty who has the final ability to overwhelm or obliterate anything He so chooses?"

Miriam added, "It was El Shaddai who said, in Genesis, to be fruitful and multiply."

Beth turned to another page and holding it up for Rachel to see, asked, "Tell me about Ehyeh asher ehyeh."

"Well, this is from the most 'famous' verses in the Hebrew bible. It is God's answer to Moses when Moses asks for God's name. God answers Moses by saying 'I will be what I will be' or some translate His answer as, 'I am that I am.' Regardless, they are powerful words. They convey His essence and nature of eternal existence and of the fact that He was the same yesterday, today, and tomorrow."

All three women sat in silence as they tried to grasp the implication of what God shared with Moses. Finally, Miriam broke the silence and suggested they warm up the coffee in their cups and sit on the balcony. Beth considered bringing the book outdoors but decided against it, as she wanted it kept safe inside.

Rachel had two pairs of wicker chairs facing each other on her balcony with a small wicker table in between each pair. In the middle of the group was a low wicker cocktail table with a glass top. Rachel sat next to Beth and Miriam took a seat opposite of them. They each put down their cups and simply enjoyed the day's breeze and sounds of activity floating up from the street. Beth had never been to pajama parties when she was young, and Sophia had always shied away from such parties, but Beth could now see why they were so popular!

Chapter Thirty

Blessed be the Lord, the God of Israel,
who alone does wonderful deeds.
Blessed be his glorious name forever;
may all the earth be filled with the
Lord's glory. Psalm 72:19

Just as the morning gave way to afternoon, so, too, their conversation gave way from the names of God to the matriarchs of the faith: Sarah, Rebekah, Rachel, and Leah. Both Miriam and Rachel were quite animated as they shared some of the teachings of these women who were referred to as 'Imahot.' Between the two of them, Beth heard how the Sabbath blessings in a Jewish home included specific blessings for a daughter, *May God make you like Sarah, Rebecca, Rachel and Leah.*

"What is a parent actually asking or saying in that blessing?" Beth asked.

"When we look at the lives of these women we see how God's hand was clearly with them," began Miriam. "Remember, Sarah, in her old age, was blessed with the birth of a beloved son and that her whole life she was considered a beautiful woman. Like Sarah, Rebekah was also beautiful. In addition, she was a kind, loving, and caring woman from whom God promised that nations would rise.

Rachel was the first in the line of matriarchs to herself approach God with her request for children and He answered her prayers with the birth of Jacob. Until that point, the men, Abraham and then Isaac, had interceded on behalf of their wives. Finally, Leah was blessed by God to give birth to so many of the tribes of Israel. All these women had God's promise, something that every mother wants for her daughter."

By late afternoon their conversation had taken another turn. Each was recalling her own special memories of Ayala, with Beth sharing her belief that God had granted her a special blessing to have known Ayala. Miriam cried in a way that seemed almost healing. She shared her inability to break down in front of her father because he very much needed her to be strong. Both Rachel and Beth understood and felt humbled that they could help their friend in such an intimate way.

At some point in the afternoon Rachel brought out a tray filled with cheeses, fruits, flat breads, and an assortment of nuts and olives. "Why don't you each go to the fridge and grab an iced tea or lemonade and I'm going to get a few warm sweaters. There's a slight chill in the evening air. Unless, of course, you would rather go back inside."

"No, this is wonderful and a heavier sweater than the one I brought would be perfect," Beth said. Miriam agreed and all three went into the apartment. Miriam and Beth walked to the fridge with Miriam selecting a raspberry iced tea and Beth settling on lemonade.

"This should fit fine," Rachel said as she returned and offered a cozy, oversized zippered sweater to Miriam. "And here's one for you," she said to Beth.

The women stood and put on their sweaters. One was a light pink and the other a light purple. Rachel's was a light green. They all looked at each other and laughed. "I have to get a camera!"

Rachel went back inside and opened a few cupboards and then shouted, "Got it!" and returned to the balcony. After a minute or two she had the camera set up on a plant stand in the corner and had positioned everyone to the best of her ability. She pushed down the automatic feature that would take the picture and ran to where she had placed Miriam and Beth. "Cheese!"

"Cheese!" the girls said as they waited with smiles on their faces. Then, when nothing happened, Rachel made a move towards the camera, at which point it flashed. Laughing hysterically, they did their best to reset both the camera and themselves. After another minute or two they were able to take a picture.

Miriam suggested a third for good measure and before long they were taking pictures of one another as well as pairs; first Beth and Miriam and then Beth and Rachel, then Rachel and Miriam. They took pictures of Beth holding her books and of Miriam hugging Rachel. They finished and Rachel promised to send copies to Beth and Miriam. Beth was glad because she hadn't spent too much time taking pictures during her trip and didn't want the entire experience to fade with time. She had purchased dozens of post-card type memorabilia but none of those had her two special friends.

Chapter Thirty-One

*May the favor of the Lord our God be
ours. Prosper the work of our hands!
Prosper the work of our hands!*
Psalm 90:17

Luke and the boys spent the morning before
Liz's return walking around the house and cleaning.
The boys were vacuuming and dusting their rooms
while Luke did the same for the living room. Luke
had Joseph shaking bathroom rugs while Sammy
washed the bathroom floors. Each was deep in
thought as the chores were being carried out.

Sophia was working. Her job at the local
library had proved to be a true blessing. She checked
books in and out and shelved returns. She had told
Luke and Liz that there were many times,
throughout the day, when she had time on her hands
and worked on her homework, scholarships, or just
plain read.

Joseph thought of how much he missed his
mom and felt a good amount of remorse at how often
he had spoken rudely to her in the past few months.
He had heard and seen his friends get away with it
and even though he knew better, he gave it his best
shot too. He knew it rattled his mom and sometimes
he found great pleasure in seeing her squirm.

The hurt would cover her face and she would
leave the room as tears welled in her eyes. *What is
wrong with me?* he silently asked himself. *What good
could come of adding grief to my mother's life?* He
made a promise to himself to do his best to stop his
mean-spirited behavior towards her and asked God to
forgive him. His mother was always telling him to

talk to God, that God would listen to him, that God was always there.

Whenever she said these things Joseph would roll his eyes, not trying to hide his disdain for his mother's constant promotion of God. Now he regretted these reactions to her and hoped God was still there to listen to him.

Luke watched Joseph pensively complete his chores and was tempted to ask him what he was thinking about. He thought better of it and didn't. It looked like Joseph was lost deep in thought and that he might be having some sort of epiphany that Luke didn't want to interrupt. He turned his attention to Sammy. Seeing that Sammy was also deep in thought, Luke gathered the laundry and made his way to the washer and dryer.

He dropped a sock or two along the way and bending down to pick them up, a shiny little light coming from under the cupboard caught his eye. Piling the clothes on top of the machine, he went to investigate. Picking up Liz's diamond earring, he remembered both of them searching high and low the previous month for it. She had dropped it when they were getting dressed for a rare night out with friends. She was heartbroken because they were a pair of earrings given to her by her grandmother. The evening had been ruined. Liz was unable to get past her heartache at having lost the earring and Luke had been quite frustrated with her at the time.

He had tried to console her, assuring her that it would turn up, but to no avail. They did everything within their power to be civil towards one another during the evening. They were, after all, with another couple. However, by the time they arrived home, the volcano had erupted and they were no longer speaking to one another. Liz did her best to sleep on the couch but finally gave in when her back began aching. Once back in bed, she lay motionless on her side, careful not to move in any way that she might inadvertently touch Luke. It took days before they began speaking again, careful to avoid the topic of the earring.

Now here he was, holding it in his hand. His heart raced as it filled with his regretful words and actions towards his wife. *How could I have treated her so unkindly? Liz has had no one in her young life who loved her except her grandmother, and I cared more about my evening than her heartache!*

Liz was a great proponent of Christ's power of forgiveness and as Luke loaded the washing machine, he found himself counting on it as he asked for Christ's hand to intervene in his marriage.

Chapter Thirty-Two

*Trust in the Lord with all your heart,
on your own intelligence rely not; In
all your ways be mindful of him, and
he will make straight your paths.*
Proverbs 3:5-6

Rachel was able to join Miriam to drive Beth to the airport. The women rode in silence. Sitting in the back seat, Beth looked out the window at the people and streets that she would always remember fondly. Unwilling to look forward and see Rachel and Miriam in front of her, Beth was reminded of when she was young and would visit her grandmother. She spent most of her holidays at her grandparent's home. They were magical for Beth, even as a teenager.

She remembered, however, the tremendous pain she would experience at the end of her time at her grandparent's. Her grandfather would drive her home and Beth would sit in the passenger seat, staring out her side window, unwilling to look forward for fear her grandfather would see her tear stained face. Each visit ended with the same torturous ride home.

Now, here she was, forty-eight years old and reliving the pain of leaving people she loved. *And to return to what? To a home filled with unhappiness and sorrow?* She wasn't sure she could bear it at this point in her life.

That was what most perplexed Beth: her children's often sour attitude. She gave them a home that was, to the best of Beth's ability, filled with love and stability. It was what Beth had always wanted and having given it to her own children, she felt as if they had rejected it in every way they possibly could; through words and through actions. From Beth's perspective, they had seemingly rejected her gifts of hearth and home. Now she was just tired.

Miriam, Rachel, and Beth arrived at the airport much sooner than Beth had hoped. *Where was traffic when you needed it?* she wondered. Rachel popped the trunk open and took out Beth's suitcases. Miriam took a place in line as the three women remained mute.

Soon Beth would be separated from Rachel and Miriam and yet words still eluded her. As she stepped forward, taking her turn to relinquish her luggage and move past security, Miriam spoke. "May the God who brought us together know our deep gratitude. And may He, blessed be His holy name, keep this special friendship in the palm of His hand."

Teary eyed, Rachel added, "May our memories of this time we had together never diminish or tarnish with age, but may they always reflect the glory of His kingdom that exists between mere humans when He so ordains."

And then together, all three women said, "Amen!" as they hugged one another for the last time. Separating, no one chose to look back, knowing that the past was a gift from God and that the future was His as well, and for that there could be no sadness.

Chapter Thirty-Three

I stretch out my hands to you; I thirst
for you like a parched land.
Psalm 143:6

Beth boarded the plane and made her way
directly to her row. She tucked her bag under the
seat in front of her and closing her eyes, put her head
back. She was next to a window and felt it was
providential as she would, undoubtedly, spend a good
amount of time looking out at the skies. Beth had
spent most of her car ride to the airport staring out
the window as well and figured this had become the
theme of the day!

Beth kept her eyes closed through the
remainder of the embarking, the pilot's information
about flight time and weather conditions, and the
flight attendants' emergency instructions. She didn't
have the energy to open her eyes and give respectful
attention to their required announcement of exit
locations and emergency procedures. She hoped that
the flight attendants weren't offended, but this was
just one of those times when Beth wanted to nurture
Beth, and opening her eyes seemed almost
impossible.

She had no appetite and was convinced it was
because her stomach was half the size it was two
weeks ago. Her eating habits had changed
drastically and she wanted to keep her new, slimmer
waist. She liked the improvement.

Soon she was sound asleep. It was a beautiful
spring day. The weather was warm, the wind
blowing gently through the newly sprouted leaves.
The sun warmed her skin and she took off her

lightweight jacket. She didn't need it as she bent down to begin work on her garden. She was inspecting last year's growth on a few bushes while deciding where to plant the early blooming larkspur plants. She loved their tall spikes and the gorgeous rose, pink, and lavender colors that she had selected. She knew what magnificent arrangments these made when cut and brought indoors and was already anticipating the centerpieces she would be able to create. She finally decided to place the larkspur behind her dwarf morning glories. She thought the contrast of heights and colors would be perfect.

As she began digging, her spade hit something hard. She bent forward to get a closer look as she used her fingers to gently pull the dirt away from the hard substance. She seemed to know that the spade would scratch or ruin whatever it was that she had discovered. Like an expert archeologist uncovering the find of the century, she brushed back the dirt to find an oval shaped rock. She picked it up and was stunned to catch a glimpse of the sun's rays reflecting off the tiniest of spots that was free from dirt. She brushed at that small spot and almost dropped the treasure when she realized that it appeared to be a diamond. She looked around to see if anyone was watching and then ran to her home.

She rushed into the small mudroom adjacent to the garage where there was a sink and ran the water over the rock. It was a diamond! As it caught the light from the ceiling, it sparkled unlike anything she had ever seen. Beth looked at the diamond and could feel the Lord speaking to her spirit, *You, my beloved Elizabeth, are like that diamond to me. You may feel that your life has covered you in mud and dirt but inside you are that precious diamond!*

Continue excavating Elizabeth. Let us work together to uncover your true, inner light.

"Ma'am! Ma'am! Are you alright?" Beth's seatmate was shaking her shoulder. Beth grudgingly woke herself up and looked at the woman who seemed so concerned. "I'm sorry but you were crying. Sobbing, really. I just wanted to make sure you were okay."

Beth stared blankly at the woman. On the one hand she felt more than a bit embarrassed to have been crying in her sleep, but on the other hand she was a bit perturbed to have been woken from the dream. This dream had been haunting her for more than a year and she finally understood its meaning! She wanted to go back to sleep and feel God speak to her spirit once more! She smiled at the woman and said, "It's been an emotional day. I guess even my subconscious is exhausted. Please forgive me."

"Oh my, don't worry! We've all been there."

For the first time Beth took in the woman's warm grayish-blue eyes and saw the sincere kindness in them. Beth smiled back and turned her head towards the window. She just knew the woman would understand.

As Beth relived her dream she also thought of her grandmother's diamond earring that she had lost over a month ago. It saddened her heart but she knew she had to let go of that ache.

Beth continued thinking of the Lord's spirit pressing upon her heart, *I am valuable!* she said to herself. She had been struggling since childhood to make that statement. With parents who had their own difficulties and needs, Beth had never been told, in words or in deeds, that she was a valuable and loved little girl. Then, as an adult, as she tried to bring these messages to her own children, they shunned her. They seemed to put little stock in what she had to offer them. Beth was finding that her life had unfolded in ways that were neither rewarding nor happy. She just didn't have any more fight left in her for her husband or her children.

Now she was seeing, through eyes of faith, what it meant to be valuable, to be a diamond! Rachel and Miriam, and even David and Meir, seemed to sincerely love having met Beth. She was warmly embraced for the woman she had become and had been validated in ways that she would never have thought possible.

Beth raised her arm to click on her reading light. She rummaged through her bag to find her reading glasses and opened her book about the Jewish matriarchs Sarah, Rebekah, Rachel, and Leah. Beth felt that these women had something very special to share and she couldn't wait to know them more completely.

Engrossed in her book, Beth was startled by the announcement that they were close to landing in New York. Where had the time gone? She leafed through the remainder of the book and was surprised that she was almost finished. She put it away and placed her reading glasses into their case before putting them away, too. Beth gazed at her seat companion, who was sound asleep, and felt grateful that she hadn't been sitting next to a 'talker.' Most of the day, Beth reflected, had been spent in silence and it was exactly what Beth had needed.

Soon they were at the terminal in New York and Beth was standing in the aisle, a bit of her old habits surfacing. In a rush to get nowhere.

Once off the plane Beth meandered through the terminal to her pre-assigned gate. Getting into her fifth line of the day, Beth began feeling agitated.

She truly did not know what to expect when she saw Luke and that uncertainty was bothering her.

She felt as if she was a different person than when she left two weeks ago. *Was that a real possibility?* she asked herself. She had to believe it was.

Beth heard her stomach rumble and decided to get out of line to purchase a salad that she could bring on the plane. Out of the corner of her eye she spotted a small café that had a large refrigerated case filled with containers that no doubt had salads and sandwiches. She made a quick beeline to the café and looked over the contents of some of the containers. There were a variety of salads and she decided on the one with mandarin oranges and slivers of chicken. She grabbed an extra package of dressing and walked to the cashier.

"That will be five dollars and seventy two cents, please."

Beth pulled out a twenty and paid the gal. Pushing her change deep into the pocket of her pants and gathering up her salad, dressing, and tote bag, Beth returned to the line. Only a few people had been checked in and Beth wasn't that far behind the first spot she had occupied, prior to getting her salad.

Boarded, Beth once again put her tote under the seat in front and placed her salad container in her lap. She knew better than to dig in before take off and then be asked to put her tray up. She decided to just wait until they were in the air before she began eating.

Very soon a young man took the seat next to Beth and eyed her salad, "Smart move."

"Yes, I slept through the meal on my last flight."

"Wow, a meal on a flight? Where were you flying from?"

"Israel," Beth said quietly.

"I've never been," he admitted, as if most people had.

"Well, I highly recommend it, if you are ever able to. It is a magnificent country filled with people from all walks of life. It is like the epicenter of the world!" Beth admitted enthusiastically.

They continued talking with Beth answering most of the young man's questions. They were well on their way before Beth finally opened her salad. The young man turned his attention to a book that looked to Beth like a college required reading. If she hadn't been so hungry she would have inquired.

Soon they were on the ground and Beth was measuring her emotions, trying to keep them in check and understand them at the same time.

Walking through the airport, she was at luggage claim in no time. People often complained about airports but Beth looked around and thought that, taking into consideration the enormity of traffic and luggage and sheer commotion, airports were actually quite impressive. The bags were on the conveyor belts within ten minutes of her arriving and she spotted hers immediately. She had tied purple ribbons on the handles because, unlike her tapestry tote bag, her luggage was very nondescript. The ribbons had been a good idea and she fielded more than a compliment or two on it.

Lifting the luggage off the belt had always cracked Beth up. It was like a comedy of errors as she did her best not to let her tote bag swing into her way while she used all her strength to hoist the bag up and over the metal edge of the conveyor, and onto the floor. More than once she had been seen running along the belt for a dozen or more feet, her laughter zapping her strength, making it impossible for her to lift her bag.

Once she had her luggage she pulled out the handle and began her walk towards the shuttle. She had never had to wait more than five minutes for her ride and today was no different. Fishing through her tote she found her parking lot ticket as well as a couple of dollar bills with which to tip the shuttle driver. About fifteen minutes later Beth was at her car.

Home sweet home, she thought. America. Land of the free. It was a beautiful country and she was grateful to be an American citizen but her eyes were now open to the world 'out there.' Was this a good or bad thing? Only time would tell. Closing the trunk, Beth walked to the driver's side of the car and got in. *Ready or not, here I come*, was all she could think.

Chapter Thirty-Four

*Glorify the Lord, Jerusalem; Zion, offer
praise to your God. Psalm 147:12*

Liz pulled her car into the garage. Everyone must have heard the garage door open because as soon as she got her luggage out of the trunk, they were all standing at the storm door, smiling. Luke was closest to the door and was reaching for the handle. He made an attempt to step forward to help with her luggage but she simply said, "I've got it." Luke gave Liz a quick, intimate kiss as she entered the house and she leaned into him for a brief embrace. She could feel his heart pounding and knew hers was also responding to their exchange.

Once she was fully inside, Sammy and Joseph threw their arms around her and said, "Welcome home, mom! We missed you. Did you have a lot of fun?"

"I missed you guys, too! And, yes, I had a whole lot of fun. I have all kinds of stories to share and post-cards for you to look at. I'm hoping you will let me spend the next week sharing them with you and sort of reliving everything. It really was amazing."

Sophia stood back while her brothers bombarded their mother with hugs and questions. When they finally released her, Sophia moved forward to hug her mother. She was relieved that Liz was home, safe and sound, and told her mother just that through tear filled eyes. The emotions in the air overwhelmed Liz, especially since they had been quite absent of late.

Luke was watching Liz hug the children. His children. Her children. He couldn't get over how very much he loved her. She smiled at him and his heart melted. "So," she began. "How is everyone doing?"

She listened as both of the boys gave her a quick run down on the latest at school and in their respective sports. Joseph was on the junior varsity hockey team and Sammy was on a school football team. "Sounds like you guys kept dad busy driving you here and there and everywhere!"

"They sure did but I didn't mind. It gave us some time together. Although I have to admit I couldn't do it all the time like you do. You have my admiration."

Sophia then shared with her mom that she had found, and began working on, the perfect scholarship application. She had also picked up a few extra hours at work and was now preparing for her mid-term exams. Liz watched her daughter talk enthusiastically about things and couldn't help but hug her. Sophia seemed to understand, for the first time, what instigated the hug and returned it.

Luke continued to watch the exchange between his wife and his children until everyone went their separate ways. Even Liz returning from another country couldn't stop them from their daily activities. When the boys finished their summary of the last two weeks, they gave their mother another big hug and went to their respective rooms. Each had pressing plans, as kids often do. Sophia, too, had obligations that she wanted to pursue. Liz and Luke stood alone in the mud room.

"Well, would you like to unpack or would you prefer to leave the luggage in the mud room and we'll go sit and have a cup of coffee?"

"Actually," Liz admitted, "a cup of coffee sounds perfect."

She washed up; wanting to get the day's traveling off her hands, and followed Luke into the kitchen. In the middle of the dining room table was a beautiful bouquet of fresh cut flowers, sitting in her favorite crystal vase. "Oh, Luke, these are beautiful," she said as she leaned in to smell the flowers. There was a card and a small box sitting in front of them. The front of the card read, *For My Precious Wife.* Liz smiled as she thought of her dream and the Spirit of the Lord pressing upon her heart that she was 'precious.' Looking at the words Luke used on the front of the card, she knew that the Lord wanted to make sure she received His message. She gave a silent prayer of gratitude.

Luke clicked on the coffee pot and had walked over to where Liz was standing. They were facing each other with no more than a few inches between them. She looked up into Luke's eyes and could see a softening that she had never noticed before. He lifted his hands to hold her face and gave her a long, sweet kiss. She felt her body respond to his and melted into his arms. They clung to each other without saying a word. Liz was finding a newfound appreciation for silence.

After a few minutes they separated and walked to the cupboard to get cups for their coffee. Luke picked the one that used to be his father's favorite. They had a set of four but no one used them except Luke. It was his special remembrance of his father, who had taught him how to enjoy a delicious cup of coffee.

Liz took the cup that had been given to her by a friend. She loved how it felt in her hand, the perfect shape and size. It had a few simple flowers on it, nothing elaborate.

Luke filled each cup and they walked into the living room, choosing to sit on the same couch. Liz had taken off her shoes in the mudroom and now tucked her feet up under herself while Luke propped his up on the ottoman in front of the couch. They were each holding their cup, more for comfort than for refreshment. It just felt good.

Luke noticed the card and box still sitting in front of the flowers, "You didn't take your presents. Let me get them for you."

He placed his coffee down and walked over to the table. He, too, leaned in to smell the flowers and picked up the card and the box. Walking back to the couch he said to Liz, "I hope you like what I have tried to say. I know you will love what is in the box."

Liz told Luke about the cup she had bought him and how it was forgotten in the commotion of the tragedy. He assured her that it was okay she had nothing to give him. He only wanted her safe return.

Beth, then, took the box from Luke's strong hand. It was a small white jewelry box that wasn't wrapped. Beth was intrigued and looked quizzically at Luke. Upon opening the lid she exclaimed, "You found it! Where did you find it?"

Luke explained to her how he had dropped some laundry and, upon picking it up, spotted the earring in a far corner. "I guess you've been right all along. I should be helping out with chores more often!" They both laughed and then she took the card from him.

Luke had only glued down a small area of the envelope so it was easy for her to open. She pulled out the card which had picture of a man and a woman, walking down the beach, holding hands. In the background the sun was setting. The sentiment inside read, *You make every day worth living.* On the left side of the card Luke had written a Scripture verse and some words in his own hand. Liz needed her glasses and went into the mud room to retrieve them. When she came back to the couch she opened the card and read:

> *Although you should be teachers by this time, you need to have someone teach you again the basic elements of the utterances of God. You need milk, not solid food. Everyone who lives on milk lacks experience of the word of righteousness, for he is a child. But solid food is for the mature, for those whose faculties are trained by practice to discern good and evil.*

> *Liz, I took the kids to church during your absence and this was the Scripture verse that was read. I felt it was so appropriate for our marriage that I wanted to share it with you. I needed to share it with you. I love you and believe that, while you are frustrated with how things are, they are really just at a mature place, as St. Paul would have said. Sure, there aren't many roller coaster ups and downs like there were in the first years of our marriage, but that's good! Please, let me convince you and help you see how very, very blessed we really are with our lives. Luke.*

Liz put the card on the table, picked up her coffee, turned to Luke and said, "Okay. Convince me." She meant it with every fiber of her being. She wanted to be convinced that her marriage, her life, was all it should and could be. She wanted something to break the shell of fear and anxiety that had already begun a convincing job of making her feel as is she had missed out on life.

She wanted Luke to counter that message with the message that life was really right here, right now, with him, with her children. Every adjective that had been thrown her way in the past few years needed to be replaced. *Could Luke do that? Could he replace 'boring' and 'failed' and 'frustrating' and 'unfulfilled' with any words, any new insights that could appease Elizabeth's restless spirit?*

Luke smiled and said "Okay. I will."

Their conversation lasted well into the night. At one point they moved from the couch to the table and Luke pulled out some tuna sandwiches that he had already prepared. In croissants, they were professionally placed on a plate of deep green, leafy romaine lettuce. Off to the side were two slices of ripe, juicy tomatoes. Liz looked at the plate and knew that if Luke hadn't been successful in his computer business, he would have been triumphant as a chef. Exhausted from her trip, she found herself quite relieved at his culinary skills.

They ate and their conversation continued. With every word, Luke conveyed his conviction that their marriage was the very thing that St. Paul chided the early believers about in Hebrews. Luke explained that the early believers were floundering and needed to be bolstered. They were weary. Not from what was happening on the outside of their faith, but from what was happening from within. There were many demands made on them as Christians, followers of Christ. Those demands were taking a toll and St. Paul sent them his encouragement.

As Luke continued he drew the comparisons to their marriage. Marriage, the institution and the daily reality of it, was demanding. It could take its toll, especially with children and jobs and dreams that did not materialize. This was how the early Christians felt. They were waiting for their Messiah to return and were losing hope. But St. Paul wanted them to be reenergized about their calling and that was what Luke wanted of Liz; to be re-energized about their marital vows. Luke shared with Liz his prayers that her trip had given her time to re-energize herself and her faith, to allow their marriage to move forward in a positive way.

There would be no fanfare; there would be no Hollywood ending. Luke laughingly told Liz he would gladly take her to a beach so she could run into his arms, but that wasn't what marriage was really all about.

As Luke talked, Liz felt her heart pound with understanding and hope. She knew he was right and felt the truth of his words seep into her soul.

"We've been together more than two decades Liz! We've had four children together, built a home, and built a business. We've been through unemployment, health crises, deaths in our extended families. We've built snowmen with the kids, nursed them through heart aches and stomach aches, and have been to the principal's office on more than one occasion! Our Christmas tree is covered with ornaments made with their precious little hands and our walls are covered with their pictures. Liz! That is better than anything anyone could ever dream up. And the best is yet to come. Let's face the future together."

Luke had three of the family photo albums out and they leafed through the pictures, amazed at the beauty of their children and how fast they had grown. Liz did not know that she was crying until Luke handed her a tissue. She wiped her eyes and looked at Luke. He was right and she knew he was right. The feelings she had sitting next to him on the couch were more powerful than anything she could read about in a book or see on television. These were real feelings based upon a life they had built together.

Luke continued, "Liz, don't get me wrong. I don't want you to give up on your dreams. I have dreams, too. But I'm saying that the unfulfilled dreams can't be a catalyst for making changes that you will regret. Think about it, if you could fill some of your most ardent dreams but not have your family, would you be okay?"

Liz shook her head. She was stuck on Luke's comments that he had dreams. She had never thought of that and was ashamed of herself. Everyone had dreams. She remembered her grandmother sharing her dreams about traveling and dancing and doing different things. Although those things never came true for her grandmother, she knew that her grandmother had no regrets. One dream, one hope, became replaced by another experience, another reality.

Luke could see that Liz was exhausted and suggested that she take a shower and climb in bed. He would do dishes and take care of her luggage. She agreed and made her way to the room. Turning on the lights, she saw that their bedroom, too, had a vase of fresh flowers. Surveying the room, she was impressed at its overall order. Luke had made sure she came home to a clean, inviting room. These were the gestures that truly mattered.

She smiled and opened her dresser to retrieve a clean set of pajamas. She walked into her bathroom and closed the door. A sense of peace enveloped her as she took her shower and then dressed. Her head wasn't on the pillow more than a few seconds before she was sound asleep.

Chapter Thirty-Five

*I know that the Lord is great; our Lord
is greater than all gods.
Psalm 135:5*

It took a few days for Elizabeth to regain her full strength after the trip. It was as if her body was putting up a good fight, not wanting to switch gears. She just slept on and off for the first full day back. Luke had taken a few days off of work and was still main caregiver to the boys and Sophia while Liz did her best to get herself together.

By the third day Liz was operating in the correct time zone and her eating was also falling in line. She didn't want dinner at breakfast and snacks in the middle of the night. Luke went back to work and Liz enjoyed having the house to herself. She did her laundry, packed away her suitcases, put her post-cards in albums, and finished reading one of the books from her trip. She wasn't expected back to work until the following Monday, which still left her with a few days to herself.

She spent a lot of her time thinking of Luke's words on her return. She loved his analogy of St. Paul's letter to the Hebrews and decided to read it from start to finish. Liz, like so many people, had read bits and pieces, here and there, but could not claim to have read any particular book of Scripture from start to finish. Even if she had, she knew her heart was now in the right place for a clearer, more meaningful understanding than at anytime before. Picking up the bible, Liz asked the Holy Spirit to imbue her with wisdom and love as she read the verses that her husband had so intimately shared with her.

Liz also filled her days with the chores she had previously felt were so mundane, responsibilities she felt were taking away from her life and not adding to it. Now, she found herself feeling quite grateful for her home and the tasks that were on her shoulders. She saw herself as an integral part of the family. She thought often of Ayala and saw how critical a mother's role was in the home. Ayala had made a beautiful home because of her love and caring for people she knew and met. Ayala wasn't famous nor had she traveled the world. But the world she traveled in was better because of her existence.

Liz remembered the 'pajama party' and thought of Rachel's explanation of the universe. Rachel had shared with Liz and Miriam that she felt the larger universe was really made up of millions of smaller ones in which people existed. Rachel's own universe, as she had expounded, consisted of her students, her family, and her friends and neighbors. What she did in that small universe greatly impacted the larger universe to which she belonged. Beth had been fascinated by Rachel's perspective but hadn't yet applied it to herself. Now, at home, she looked around at her universe and was in awe. She thought of the mother and son on the flight to Israel and understood the significance of Rachel's words.

Liz had always wanted to know that her life made a difference and was seeing, as if for the first time, how very much it truly mattered. She was irreplaceable to her husband and her children. She was a daughter and a friend. She was a teacher and a co-worker. All of a sudden, Liz's universe was bigger and more dramatic than she had ever imagined.

Although she and Luke had not had any more in-depth conversations, they were respectful and cordial in a loving, almost newlywed sort of way. That first night together, when Liz read Luke's card and then they talked for hours, had been more productive than all their time at the counselor's. But to be fair, Liz thought, the sessions at the counselor's could have helped put both her and Luke in the right frame of mind for this step in their marriage.

Dinners with the kids were quiet and made Liz think of her peaceful silence with Miriam and Rachel. At one point, not too long before, she had found silence at the dinner to be maddening. She envisioned that every family dinner should be alive with conversation, witty banter, and gregarious tales of the day's events. She had a whole new appreciation for silence and now felt blessed just to be at the table with her husband and children.

Other things were changing too. Luke made more of an effort to acknowledge her contributions to the family. He continued to be a major force, strong in his opinions, but seemed to realize that Liz was also as dynamic as he was and that he had to make provisions for her interests, her ways.

There seemed to be no change in the children's bickering except that she now listened with less intensity. Whereas before each unkind word they spewed at one another felt like a stab in Liz's heart, she now made a conscious effort to release herself from feelings of failure. When Sophia stormed out of a room because of her brother's 'lameness,' Liz tried to shrug it off. Her children were not perfect, nor could she expect them to be. The kids knew, however, the family rules, morals, and expected behavior. Liz began making a conscious effort to remind herself that she was, indeed, doing a fine job as their mother, even if she didn't always see the rewards.

By her second week home, and her return to work, Liz's perspective was slowly but steadily changing. She was feeling a renewed sense of purpose in her life as a woman, wife, and mother. Her friends became nearer and dearer to her. She felt blessed because God gave her the grace to see her life as His gift, not in what it didn't have but in what it did have. And she was seeing that it had so much!

Writing a test for her science students, she also had a renewed sense of direction. For the past few years she had bemoaned her low salary and ever-increasing demands. Now, with her oldest son in college, she recognized her work as a way to help her students achieve their own goals and dreams. *How fortunate to be in this position!* she found herself thinking. She thought of Rachel and began looking at her classroom like a universe. Through her own actions as a teacher and co-worker she could make positive contributions to the bigger world.

Friday evening, towards the end of her second week at home, she sat and composed letters to Meir, Miriam, and Rachel. She had no way to contact David and simply enclosed a note to him in Meir's envelope. She did the same with a note to Sipporah in Rachel's envelope. In some ways she wanted to ensure that her time in Israel had not been a dream. It seemed so long ago and so far away. She chuckled when she thought it had been in an entirely different universe!

That night Liz and Luke went out to dinner and a movie. They enjoyed one another's company and talked of their thoughts about the future. Luke shared his dreams and Liz listened. She hesitated to share hers as she realized that Luke was well aware of most of her hopes and dreams as well as her disappointments and regrets.

Nonetheless, he encouraged her and she shared with him her continued interest in teaching at the local community college. Luke helped her sketch out a plan for her continued education and together they came up with some ideas of people she could contact and things she could do. Like her trip to Israel, she realized that half the fun was in the planning. She knew that even if she never became a college professor, she would always cherish this particular conversation with her husband.

The next morning Liz heard the mail truck round the corner and pulled on her coat. She picked up the letters from the counter to walk them to the mailbox. She wanted to get them in the day's mail. To her surprise, the mail carrier was at her door. Liz smiled at her and then felt the flutter of her heart as she saw the box the carrier was holding, neatly packaged and taped, postmarked from Israel. There was also a thick envelope with a return address from Rachel. Taking the box and the envelope, Liz almost forgot about her own letters. "I'm sorry," Liz called to the carrier as she was half way back down the driveway. "Could I please give these to you?" Liz ran to catch up with her and gave her the letters.

Back in the house, Liz picked up the package and walked into the mud room, looking for a pair of scissors. Luke was doing a few errands and each of the boys was occupied, one with a social studies paper and the other with a game on the computer. Sophia was at work. For all intents and purposes, Liz had the house to herself.

Cutting through the packing tape, she opened the box. It was filled with a myriad of packing materials to ensure the safety of the contents. There was bubble wrap along with rolled up newspaper, squished in between bits of styrofoam. Carefully removing the protection, she began to uncover the pieces to the tea set. One by one, she lifted out the cups. Each so beautifully painted and magnificent to behold. She then came across a flat piece of cardboard that had created a bottom section to the box. Lifting it, Liz saw this section was as safely packed as the first. David and Miriam took no chances with the set! Again, gently removing the packing materials, she caught a glimpse of the tea pot. Lying there, in all its beauty, Liz gazed upon it and began to weep.

She thought of her own ongoing dream, so vivid in her mind, of gardening and unearthing the diamond. She thought of Ayala, a kindred soul whom she had only known for a matter of days but who had impacted her life as if Liz had known her always. She cried for her grandmother, whom she dearly missed, and for the broken relationship with her best friend that had never been resolved. Liz wept in gratitude for her children and her husband and her friends. Finally, she cried with the knowledge that God's graces had never left her life.

Wiping her eyes, Liz gathered a few pieces of the tea service and the envelope which she knew contained the pictures that Rachel had promised to send, and walked into the kitchen. Setting everything down on the counter, she put on water to boil. She then went back into the mud room to get the remaining tea set pieces and returned to the kitchen. Rummaging through her cupboards for the perfect tea, she selected a honey almond flavor. Once her tea was made, she picked up her beloved books and settled herself into her favorite chair. She set her tea cup and its saucer on the small end table and clicked on the lamp. She had the envelope tucked under her arm and placed it on the table by her tea. The sun's rays were making their way through the clouds and into the room. Liz felt that the Lord was reaching out to her. She raised her tea cup in the air and said to her Creator, "Shabbat Shalom."

Resources and Reflections for Readers

Chapter One

My deepest appreciation to Morris Rosenthal for his unending patience as I plied him with questions! Please consider visiting his website www.fonerbooks.com for information regarding Jerusalem.

Chapter Two

Yom Kippur is the highest of holy days for Jews. It is the Day of Atonement. According to Leviticus, there are seven feasts throughout the year that God's people are called to celebrate (see Leviticus 23, Exodus 12:37a, Numbers 28:16-29:40). Four of these feasts are in the spring (Pesach, Hag HaMatzah, Sfirat HaOmer, and Shavuot). The remaining three are in the fall and along with Yom Kippur include Rosh HaShana and Sukkot.

Chapter Three

Read and meditate upon Romans 11:21-24 in which St. Paul makes it clear that Gentiles are grafted to the olive tree only through God's grace and mercy. Spend time in gratitude for the ways in which God gives you His grace which allows you to stand in faith.

Chapter Four

Shalom means "peace." It is also part of the name Gideon gave to the altar in Judges 6:24; Jehovah-Shalom, the Lord sends peace. How does your life reflect God's peace? In what ways do you need to more readily accept and give Christ's peace in your daily walk?

Chapter Five

1 Samuel tells the story of King Saul's son Jonathon and Jonathon's friendship with David. It shares with us the value of anointed friendships, which are truly gifts from God. Consider, with gratitude, the friendships God has given you that enrich your journey.

Chapter Six

Proverbs 20:23 states the Lord is appalled by unfair business practices. Ask God to reveal to you ways in which your dealings with others have grieved Him. If need be, consider ways in which to provide a remedy.

Chapter Seven and Nine

Genesis 2:2 and Exodus 20:8 call man to observe the Sabbath and keep it holy. In what ways do you honor this command? In what ways to do you need to make changes? For Jews the Sabbath begins at sundown because the story of creation begins with night and then day. It begins with chaos and then order. To this day, Jews observe Sabbath from Friday sundown to Saturday sundown.

Chapter Eight

The Jerusalem Post, Christian Edition can be found online at . . . http://info.jpost.com/C006/ChristianEdition/

Chapter Ten

If you have children, consider ways in which you can spend time with them that is different from your daily or weekly routine. Find a good movie to see together, a good book to read aloud, or in some way share time with your children that is unique. Invite God into the experience and thank Him for the ways He has blessed your home.

Chapter Eleven

There are many different delicious falafel recipes. Here is just one . . .

Ingredients: 8 oz chick peas; 1 onion, very finely chopped; 1 garlic clove, crushed; 2 tablespoons minced cilantro; 1 tsp. coriander, ground; 1/4 tsp. cayenne; 1 tsp. cumin; 3 tbsp parsley, finely chopped; Kosher salt, to taste; oil for frying.

Preparation: Soak the chick peas overnight; Cover with plenty of fresh water and cook for 1 - 1 1/2 hours until tender; Blend the drained, cooked chick peas and all spices to a purée; Let the mixture rest for 1-2 hours, then roll between the palms into firm 1" balls; Heat oil (at least 1 inch deep) in a pan and fry the balls, a few at a time, until nicely brown all over — about 2-3 minutes.

Chapter Twelve

Spend time reading Isaiah 53 and reflect on the goodness of the Lord who sent His son for our transgressions.

Chapter Thirteen

Consider what 2 Corinthians 6:16-18 means to you. While we are called to love our neighbors, in what ways must we separate ourselves from what is happening around us?

Chapters Fourteen, Fifteen, Sixteen, and Twenty-Three

It is considered by both Old and New Testament standards that burying the dead is a good deed. Catholics consider it a Corporal Act of Mercy while Jews consider it a mitzvah. This is because, as Christ has taught, doing something for someone who cannot repay you is the ultimate good deed. Consider ways in which you can help at your church or a local funeral home by offering food or your services, anonymously, to a grieving family.

Chapter Seventeen, Eighteen, Nineteen, Twenty-One, and Twenty-Two
For information on Israel's beautiful sights, http://www.goisrael.com/tourism_eng. Also, if you are interested in Miriam's 'incident,' please watch for the release of "Miriam" in the late fall of 2007 from Bezalel Books.

Chapter Twenty
There are many excellent recipes for Tabouli. Here is one to try that serves around 5 . . .

3/4 cup boiling water or chicken stock; 1/2 cup cracked wheat or fine bulgur; 1/2 cup minced parsley; 1/4 cup minced mint leaves; 1/2 cup finely chopped green onion; 1 tomato, diced; 1 cucumber, seeded and diced; 3 tablespoons olive oil; 2 tablespoons lemon juice; 1 tsp. kosher salt

Pour boiling water over the cracked wheat, cover, and let stand about 20 minutes until wheat is tender and water is absorbed. Add the chopped vegetables and toss to mix. Combine oil or substitute, lemon juice, salt, pepper, and allspice. Add to wheat mixture and mix well. Serve warm or chilled. (My family loves this, made without the chicken stock, with a scoop of tuna on top for Fridays during Lent!).

Chapter Twenty
Ephesians 3:19 states that we are no longer strangers and sojourners, but fellow citizens with the household of God. Mediate upon this grace and share your gratitude with God.

Chapter Twenty-Four
Write a marriage prayer for all your friends and family. In the prayer, name the couples as you raise them

Elizabeth

to God and ask for His blessings upon their homes and in their relationships. Add this prayer to your daily prayers.

Chapter Twenty-Five

Many thanks to Joel Chernoff of the Messianic Jewish Alliance of America for permission to use information from their website. For more information, please visit . . .http://www.mjaa.org/.

Chapter Twenty-Six and Thirty

Marriage is often quite different than we expect. It requires more commitment, more perseverance than most of us realize. In my book, "Reclaiming Your Christian Self in a Secular World: A Woman's Bible Study," the chapter on Zipporah focuses in on this reality. The book also studies Sarah, Rebekah, and Rachel as matriarchs of our faith. Please visit my website www.AskKnockSeek.com for more information.

Chapter Twenty-Seven

We often forget that while our journeys are somber, they are also gifts from God and meant for our enjoyment. Find ways in which your spirit can be renewed through the joys of enjoying the life given to you by God.

Chapter Twenty-Eight

My favorite coffee website is www.Beanstro.com.

Chapter Twenty-Nine

There are many excellent books and websites on the names of God. I found this one interesting with the names in Hebrew http://www.ldolphin.org/Names.html.

Chapter Thirty-One

Spend time studying Scripture verses on forgiveness and allow God to speak to you through these verses: 2 Timothy 3, Luke 23:24, Matthew 18:21-35.

Chapter Thirty-Two and Thirty-Three

In the hustle and bustle of your everyday life, set aside time to hear the still, small voice of God: 2 Kings 2:1-2, 6-14, Luke 9:51-62.

Chapter Thirty-Four

Spend time with some of the following Scripture verses on family: Genesis 18:19, Joshua 24:15, Jeremiah 29:4-6, Matthew 18:19-20, Acts 16:30-33.

Chapter Thirty-Five

May Christ's peace be with you!